Awakening: A Willow Creek Vampires Novel
STEPHANIE SUMMERS

DISCARD

Awakening
© 2014, 2015 Stephanie Summers.

Published by: Wicked Dragon Publishing

PROLOGUE

From nothing, a swirling mist of consciousness began to form. The sweet relief of darkness faded, giving way to light. A man—an ancient man with dark curls framing a hardened face. His lips curled into a sinister smile while dark brows drew closer together. A tremendous pressure built in the air, holding him in place, as the man moved closer. The man began to speak, though his words fell on deaf ears. Eyes as dark as coal peered through the abyss revealing... something... a familiar abomination. But who was he and why did he seem so close in the nothingness?

With an icy touch, unfamiliar and unbridled power coursed through Remy's veins, restoring life as it went. Fangs elongated as hunger, so intense it threatened to uncage the beast buried within, consumed him. The scent of love grew faint as he hungered to taste the sweet blood responsible for the assault on his senses. Heavy lids opened, revealing dark eyes that were once vivid and bright like emeralds.

Awakening, he sprang to his feet, looking around at the crowd of humans. Teeth bared, he was ready to take every last drop of life from them all until he could find the source of the only blood, he knew, would entirely satiate the thirst that felt as if it had been building for centuries. Beating hearts and voices pounded through his ears while silence gave way to sound. Chaos ensued as a crowd full of newly turned humans tried to make sense of the events that had transpired.

Men and women scrambled about. Some of them wailed from utter panic while others barely moved from shock.

Bastian, the former lord of the manor, stood at the center of them with a cold, hardened look about him. Hands grasped at his legs, begging him to fix everything, but he could not, for he was merely human as well.

To his left, the only vampire remaining in the crowd shielded a young woman. Shifter, he quickly decided from the poorly masked scent tangled with magic she emitted.

A few of the humans began to notice Damen—or at least that was what he thought his name was. Damen drew their attention because he wasn't reacting and still had the brilliant eyes of a vampire. They moved toward him, pleading for him to turn them back into immortal beings. Body stiffening as his eyes narrowed, Damen's gaze landed on him.

Searching for the source of the feminine scent of love or a glimpse of the one who had left it behind, he scanned the room, but she was nowhere to be found. The noise level rose, making his head throb.

"Silence!"

The crowd stilled. He walked swiftly to the center of the room where Bastian stood.

"Remy, my son, please let us sit and discuss this. We need each other now more than ever. Let us put the past behind us."

Remy, yes, that was his name.

2

"Your son?" Remy dragged his hand through his hair and stepped closer to Bastian, forcing him to stumble back a step. "Do you not realize what has happened," he said, his head tilting to the side, "mortal?"

"I know we have all lost our immortality because you foolishly chose to kill Nicas," Bastian said, never losing his composure.

"Not all of us. Damen is still vampire. I am still vampire. And, you? You are *nothing*. How does it feel to have your fate in my hands once again? How does it feel to have to obey *me* if you want to live?"

Bastian's eyebrows knitted together as he studied Remy's face. "My son... once again?"

"I am *not* your son. You should never have summoned me here or allowed this to happen."

"If I had not summoned you, she would never have existed to you. Is that something you would throw away so easily? I know I would not."

Remy turned to Damen, motioning him forward. "A king should have a proper seat to sit upon. Go to this old fool's room and search through his collection of useless garbage until you find something fitting. Then, find *her*. She must return to me immediately." *What was her name? Ah, yes, they mentioned the name Sabine while babbling on about nothing, just before... That must be her.*

Within a few minutes, Damen came back hauling a gaudy chair adorned with golden accents and a black velvet seat. He sat it on the raised platform, and peered at the crowd of quiet humans.

Remy lifted Bastian by the throat. Gasping for air, his legs kicked as he tried to squirm out of Remy's cold grasp. "I believe a little poetic justice is in order. Take him to the dungeon where he held me."

Remy tossed Bastian aside like a rag doll and placed himself on the throne.

CHAPTER 1

Sabine Crowley slammed the car into park and exited, making her way quickly through the front door. Heavy breaths echoed through the hallway as she hurried to the ballroom to see what awaited her. The coolness of the marble floors soothed her scratched and dirtied bare feet. The only regret she had from rushing out earlier was that she didn't stop to put on shoes... Well, that and leaving her beloved's corpse sprawled out on a cold, marble floor.

Tears threatened to wet her cheeks as she prepared to see Remy lying dead where she'd left him only a few hours before. A flash of fear rippled through her body. *I really shouldn't have come back here. I'm a Grade-A dumbass. I know it's a trap. If it wasn't, why wouldn't Sam or Damen just tell me what was up? Or even Gretchen, for that matter? I should've just left town.*

Hesitating at the entrance of the ballroom, she took a deep breath and pushed the doors open. A crowd of humans—once vampires—knelt with their backs toward her. Glancing to the spot where she'd left her love lying, her stomach knotted as the air, thick and stifling, closed in around her, threatening to take her breath away. The absence of his body tore through her like a bullet to the heart, hurting so much more than she'd anticipated. Trying to hold back the tears with a trembling lower lip, she sniffled once and looked in the direction everyone faced. Swallowing hard, she tried to calm her nauseated stomach.

A glint of gold caught her eye, drawing her gaze to a large, ornate chair sitting on the raised platform. The same raised platform where she'd married Remy and almost been forced to marry Bastian not that long ago. Someone sat in the chair, but it wasn't Damen like she'd expected.

Her gaze landed on the face of the one vampire she longed to see. He'd showered and changed out of the ratty, old jeans he'd been imprisoned in. He wore boots, a clean pair of jeans that hung perfectly on his masculine frame, and a gray, just-tight-enough V-neck T-shirt. His hair, pulled back loosely, exposed his chiseled jaw.

Gasping, she cried out, "Remy!"

Taking off as fast as she could toward him, the tears she'd tried to keep from falling streamed down her face and dripped onto her chest. He stood as she approached him. Throwing her arms around his neck, she hugged him as tight as she could, vowing never to leave his side again.

As she crashed into him, his body bowed slightly to accommodate the difference in height as she threw her arms around him, but stayed mostly still. His hands barely grazed her shoulders while he inhaled deeply. She expected him to embrace her, not sniff her like a dog. This wasn't a man acting as if he'd just come back from the dead who was eager to see his wife again. His touch was indifferent, at best.

She pulled back, looking intently at him. "What's wrong with you?" Noticing his abnormally dark eyes, she tried to process everything that had happened over the last thirty seconds.

"There is nothing wrong with me." He let go of her and sat down, peering up at her as he rested his chin on his fist. "I'm better than I've been in centuries. I've brought you back here because you belong to me, and I wanted to gaze upon my possession once more."

"What?" Her mouth dropped open slightly as she took a step back.

His eyebrow cocked in annoyance. "Did I stutter?"

"What's happened to you?" she whispered.

"Damen, see that she gets to her room. I'll be in shortly to speak with her. Just as soon as I figure out what to do with this lot," he said, nonchalantly waving a hand toward Bastian's former wedding guests.

"No," Sabine exclaimed. Fists balling at her sides, her mouth set in a straight line. "You aren't just going to brush me off like that. Quit being an asshat. Now answer me, what is wrong with you?"

His jaw clenched as he glared at her. "I'll be there in a few minutes. Go now before you get yourself into real trouble." The gaze from his cold eyes nearly turned her to ice.

She turned and stormed out of the room, Damen and Sam following closely behind. None of them spoke a word until they were safely in her library.

Sabine and Sam took one another's hand and both grabbed hold of Damen as they entered so that he could see them. The witch, Mary Mercy, had taught Sabine a cloaking spell for this room that would keep her hidden and protected from anyone she needed to get away from. Sam had performed the same spell to keep herself hidden while she helped Sabine in the weeks leading up to where they presently found themselves.

"Tell me what the hell is going on," Sabine demanded, pushing a few stray hairs out of her face.

"He's different. I don't know how, but he is. Before he sent Bastian down there," Damen said, pointing down at the floor toward the dungeon beneath the room, "I asked how he'd been revived. He confided in me that he absorbed all of Nicas' power when he killed him, and that he had Nicas to thank for everything. He spoke about Nicas as if he were a god." Damen paced back and forth across the room before settling his back against the wall. "I honestly have no clue what to do. This is not something that has ever happened before. For all I know, he and I are the only two vampires left in the world."

"Are you okay?" Sam asked, wrapping her arms around Sabine.

"I'm in shock, mostly. I don't understand why he acted like he didn't care about me at all... Why didn't you tell me what I was walking into?"

"Because, at first, we thought it would be a huge surprise for you," Damen said, glancing at Sam with a look of concern in his eyes. "I sensed he was a little different, but figured it was because he was dead right before that. I mean, how can being dead not make you a little off your rocker if you manage to come back? As time went by, and you didn't respond to either of our texts, I didn't want to alarm you any further by telling you he wasn't right. I'd hoped once he saw you, he'd be more like himself again."

"I've lost everything if I lose him." She sobbed into Sam's shoulder. She didn't want to be, and never thought she'd be, one of those girls whose whole life revolved around a man, but she'd sort of been thrown into that type of situation by default when she was chosen on her eighteenth birthday.

"You have me." Sam squeezed her tight.

"I know, I do. Thank you. I don't mean to sound ungrateful for your friendship. It's just that my family is gone." Trembling, she gripped Sam's arm and pulled her closer. "I needed to go home, but home was for sale, and they didn't even tell me they left. I thought Remy was dead, and to walk in and see him up there, only to have him act as if he doesn't care... I'm so lost."

Letting loose of Sam, she moved to her reading chair and sat down, pulling her knees up to her chest. A vacant look spread across her face as she looked out the bay window at nothing. The door to the room opened, catching Sabine's attention only a few moments later.

Remy stepped through the door, and annoyed didn't even begin to describe the look on his face. His features were hardened and intense as he surveyed the room. He stood tall, crossing his arms as he said, "I know you're here. I can smell you. You need to show yourself now."

Damen stiffened and turned to Remy. "Just give her a minute, man. Christ."

"You need to leave, Damen. We'll chat soon. That goes for you, too, little shifter. I know you're mucking about in here as well. I wouldn't try to get on my bad side right now if I were you."

Sabine stood and walked out of the room. Entering the bedroom, she sat patiently on the bed, waiting for him. Sam nodded and mouthed, "I'm here for you" as she made her way to the bedroom door, Damen following close behind with his hand resting on the small of her back.

"She's in here, your royal fucking highness," he said before leaving.

In an instant, Remy stood before her. She swallowed hard and longed for him to take her into his arms and tell her he loved her; that it was all just an act to fool everyone for some reason he'd explain and it would all make perfect sense. For the first time in weeks, bars didn't separate them, and they were free to do as they pleased, yet she felt further away from him than she ever had before.

"You must have some questions. I will try to answer them the best I can if you can manage to behave yourself and not act like a child."

She fought the urge to sigh and make some show of how annoyed she was with his comment, but decided to ignore it. That would only prove his point. *How would he act if he were me?*

"Why are your eyes so dark? Are you in some perpetual state of pissed off?"

"I hadn't realized they were." Looking in the mirror hanging on the wall, he checked things out for himself. He studied his reflection as if it were the first time he'd really looked at his features before. "I suppose it has to do with the power coursing through my body."

She stood and took a step toward him. "Do you still love me?"

"Love?" He shook his head slightly. "I feel nothing for you except lust for your blood."

"You told me I was the love of your life and to never forget it, so why have you forgotten it so easily?" She turned her back to him, placing her hands on the top of a writing desk to brace herself for the answer.

"I'm afraid I'm not the same vampire you fell in love with. The Remy you knew was weak, always quietly brooding and longing for love while putting on a devil-may-care attitude to cover it up, but no more." He stepped back, eying her. "Sabine, my darling, please turn around so I can get a better look at you."

Her name rolling off his tongue taunted her. Ignoring his request, she sat down on the bed. As she held her head in her hands, tears ran down her face, dripping onto the floor below. "I don't understand any of this."

"It's really quite simple. He died... trying to save you from the life you'd been sentenced to with Bastian. He succeeded in that, but he had to pay the price."

11

She calmed for a moment, pushing the tears away, as something about the way he spoke caught her attention. "Why are you referring to yourself like you're talking about someone else?"

He hesitated for a moment before answering. "To ease your pain. I refer to him because, as I said before, I am not the vampire you fell in love with. It's best for you to mourn him so we can move on with whatever arrangement, or *relationship* if you prefer, we choose to pursue."

She stood and took his face in her hands. His skin felt like she was touching a statue. Cold and unmoving. "I won't mourn *you*. Maybe it'll just take some time for you to get back to normal. You didn't feel right at first after Mary did that spell to separate you from Bastian," she said, looking at him with hope in her eyes. If she could just convince him that the problem was something simple that she could help him fix, then this nightmare could be over and done with. They could get on with their life together and leave this little hiccup far behind.

He brushed her hands away from him and rolled his eyes. "So naïve."

"Being hopeful is not the same as being naïve. Just let me go if you aren't willing to give it some time."

"I can't do that, not yet anyway. I have to figure all of this out. There is still technically the arrangement between the vampire lord of this town and its people. Since I am the lord of all vampires and happen to be here right now, I must accept the obligation. I have to decide if it's worth staying here or not. If I decide to leave, I may let you go, but I might just take you along."

"What's the point?" she asked, plopping herself down on the bed.

"You smell positively divine and the thought of tasting your blood drives me insane." His canines sharpened into points as he swallowed hard and stared a hole right through her throat.

"Oh, my blood... That, you remember..." She watched the first sign of desire spread over his face since she'd found him alive, but it wasn't for her. Not really. Her blood was purely responsible this time. "Drain me now, and let me die in peace. Take one last taste of me, and let me go."

"Are you always this dramatic?" He threw his hands into the air and let them fall to his sides.

Um, yeah, did he just meet me today? Before she had a chance to respond, he sat beside her and leaned into her personal space. His scent, masculine and heady, caressed her nose like a beautiful nightmare.

"I'm not going to kill you, and I don't understand why you think I would."

"Because I mean so little to you now, and you're apparently some sort of fucking Dracula—being King of Vampires and all. No, wait... Even Dracula was capable of loving, so I guess you're just a monster."

"Did you truly love him?" Cocking his head slightly to the side, he studied her and the anger that coursed through her body.

She brought her hand to her chest and inhaled deeply. His words tore through her like a knife. "How can you...? Why would you ask me that? Of course, I did... I still do. I still love you." Turning away from him, her lip quivered as a tear slid down her reddened cheek. "It's why my blood is so fucking enticing to you or did you forget that, too?" she asked, voice cracking on the last word.

"How easily you throw around childish names for the one you claim to love. I am not a monster, or whatever it was you called me earlier—an asshat, I believe. Your time with me doesn't have to be as miserable as you seem to think it will be. I can show you the world and all its wonders and treasures."

The time they'd spent in Europe for the better part of a year flashed through her mind. That trip had meant everything, not only to her, but to him as well. His choice of words confused her. He'd already shown her more of the world and its wonders than she ever thought she'd see.

"Would a monster plan to reward your shifter friend for all the help she provided us? I have to admit, I never would have believed a shifter would be so helpful to our kind, but Damen was adamant that she wasn't a threat and had always been our friend. He seemed a little smitten with her. To each their own, I suppose."

"How do you not remember that she helped us to begin with? You were always in on the plan. You fed from her numerous times to rebuild your strength. And you've already shown me part of the world. Don't you remember any of our time together?"

"The time line of events have become fuzzy for me, though some of the memories are becoming clearer… I haven't quite figured out what I will do, but I will reward her somehow. I don't think that is the action of a monster."

He still isn't acknowledging our trip... "Buy her a home and release her mother from being an offering. She has no home and no family."

"Hm. I'll keep that in mind. Maybe I should make you my queen and have you as a consultant as well as a warm body to fuck whenever we feel like it."

She breathed deeply and sighed. "No," she said, shaking her head.

"No? Are you not still my wife according to vampire law? Technically, you *are* my queen, and as much as you want to try right now and act like you loathe what I've become, I can hear your heart skip a beat when I say that I still want to fuck you."

"I want no part of it. Maybe if you were still you, but you aren't you. I don't appreciate you speaking to me like that either."

"Fine. I'll leave you be for now, though I should warn you, I can feel the thirst growing again. You know how wonderful that will feel for you, so you'd better prepare yourself. I indulged on a few more humans than I should have before you came back, which is the only reason I haven't had a taste of you already.

Unfortunately, none of them tasted as good as I expect you to taste, but I am thoroughly stuffed, so it'll have to wait."

She walked into the bathroom and slammed the door shut. Staring straight ahead at nothing, she leaned against the wall and slid to the floor.

My blood... It's always been so sweet to him, the best he's ever had because of the feelings I have for him, so why now does he talk about it like he's never tasted it before? What the actual fuck is wrong with him, and how the hell am I going to fix him?

CHAPTER 2

A light tap came from the other side of the bathroom door.

"Sabine?"

"It's not locked."

The door slowly creaked open as Sam entered. She sat down beside Sabine and draped her arm over her shoulders.

"You okay?"

Her head shook ever so slightly. "So much has changed, and I can't wrap my brain around any of it. He's gone, yet he's here... taunting me."

"I wish I could make it better."

"Me too, but Sam, I'm starting to think you should get out of here while you still can. He claims he means you no harm and that he's grateful for your help, but I can't really trust that he won't hurt you."

"I'm not leaving you. You're my friend, one of the only real ones I've ever had. I'm not leaving you behind." The two girls hugged one another.

"I know you want to help, but if you and your mother get a chance to get out of her, take it."

Sam nodded and forced a half-smile. "Maybe Mary could do something to help you forget or get over him faster. Or Damen..."

"I don't want to forget him or what we had. It was too important to just give it up, and it deserves to be mourned if this is how things have to be."

"So, will you try to get through to him?"

"I just know I can't give up on him completely. There still has to be a part of him deep down that remembers what we had and feels it."

"You amaze me, woman."

Sabine chuckled and looked at Sam. "Oh, yeah?"

"Yeah. Most people would just say 'screw him' and move on... but not you."

"It might be a little easier to do that if I weren't basically a prisoner."

"I'm so sorry. Try to have faith that it'll all work itself out. I know how awful that sounds right now, but you have to just believe that he will come back to you."

"You are a downright awesome person, you know that? I wish we'd met sooner."

"Well, we aren't old or anything, you know." Sam took her arm away from Sabine and playfully jabbed her in the ribs with her elbow. "We have our whole lives ahead of us... Hopefully, they'll be really long lives." Sam giggled.

"Oh, Sam!" *I can't believe I almost forgot! Might as well have something good happen today to make up for all the bad shit.* Grabbing Sam's hand, she stood and dragged her along behind her through the door. "Let's go!"

"Where?"

"You'll see!"

A few moments later, Sabine poked her head into the entertainment room, smiling brightly at the woman sitting in the chair.

"Hi! I'm so glad you're still awake. I was afraid you'd gone to bed already since it's pretty late. I have someone I want you to meet."

Samantha put down her book and sat up. "Too much going on to sleep. After all the shenanigans happening earlier, I'd love to meet someone sane." She laughed.

Pulling Sam through the door, Sabine presented her to the woman she believed to be Sam's mother.

Samantha smiled as she looked at Sam. Eyes glistening, she hesitated before speaking. "Have we met before? You seem so... familiar."

"Samantha, this is Sam." Sabine said, pushing her forward a little.

Samantha stood and stepped closer to Sam. "My Sammy? My baby?" She gasped, tears flowing down her face. Her body jerked as she tried to hold the sobs back. Reaching out, she grabbed the back of the chair to steady herself.

"Mom?" Blinking rapidly, Sam peered at Sabine before studying the woman's face.

Nodding, Sabine said, "Yes, she's your mother."

Sam launched herself into her mother's arms, breathing her in. She hadn't been there since she was a baby, but it felt so natural. Like it was where she was meant to be. Sabine quietly left the room and gave them some time alone together.

"How?" Samantha asked, wiping tears away from Sam's cheeks. "How are you here?"

"Sabine... I told her I had a mother who was an offering, and she figured out it was you. I thought you were dead." Sam buried her face against her mother's chest, relishing the feel of her embrace. Her whole life she had longed to be in her mother's arms just once and now, it was finally happening. "Granny and Pap told me you died. They never even told me your name."

"I'm right here, sweetheart. I never thought I'd see you again."

* * *

Sabine listened in the hallway for a minute before heading back to her room. Sam knew where to find her, and Sabine thought they needed the time together without her gawking at them.

Her stomach rumbled, reminding her that she hadn't eaten at all that day. She made her way to the kitchen where a feeding frenzy was taking place. Apparently, humans who used to be vampires really managed to work up an appetite. Where the kitchen staff would get enough food to actually feed everyone in such a short period of time was a detail she didn't feel like pondering for more than a couple seconds. She had too many other things running through her mind, and she had no desire to mingle with former vampires.

Moving on toward the front of the house, she noticed people milling about and setting up makeshift beds for themselves on floors, couches, and any flat, empty spots they could find.

Um, ok. Why the hell aren't these people leaving? They can't all just move in here. Most of them would have left after the ceremony anyway, so why are they still here?

If she couldn't eat in peace, at least she could get a moment of solitude under the moonlight. She longed to be back under her favorite willow tree in her parent's yard. Its swaying branches always calmed her, allowing her to work out some of the toughest issues she'd faced. Just being outside would have to do.

The night air of summer filled her lungs. She inhaled deeply, hoping to relax by herself in the fresh air for a moment. Unfortunately, a slew of people gathered out there as well.

Huffing, she turned and headed for her room. It was late, and she hadn't slept at all. *Might as well just go to bed. I can eat when I wake up and there shouldn't be anyone trying to sleep in my room.* She also hadn't even managed to change out of her "wedding" dress. Thankfully, though ornately designed, it was only a white halter dress that was similar to the sundress she wore frequently.

As she turned a corner on her way back, she ran smack dab into Remy.

"I was just looking for you, Sabine." Taking her hand in his, he said, "Come with me."

She quickly jerked her hand away. "I'd rather not." When she tried to step around him, he blocked her way.

"I don't believe I gave you an option."

Turning, he glanced over his shoulder to make sure she was following him. They walked down the hall and into the room they'd shared. He closed the door behind them.

"You should know Bastian is imprisoned below this room. Fitting, don't you think?"

"I'd say losing his immortality is probably punishment enough, though I'm not the one to judge him. If you're planning to keep him alive, don't forget he can't survive down there without food and water."

"Oh, so now you're concerned for his well-being? After he locked me down there and tried to steal what was mine? Maybe you didn't mind being with him so much after all."

Sighing, she sat herself down. "What does any of that matter now? You don't love me anymore. You said so yourself, or was that a lie?"

"I have no reason to lie."

"Ok, then you have no reason to be upset."

"You are mine. He had no right." When he thought about her being with Bastian, a feeling of rage churned deep in his gut, fighting to break through. He pushed it away as soon as he felt it.

"I'm a person, not a goddamn possession. I'm so sick of hearing I 'belong'…"

Cutting her off with a change of subject, he said, "I'm sure you've noticed how crowded our home has become. That's why I will be staying here with you. I had thought about taking Bastian's quarters, but all my things are still here, and we need his rooms to help house all of these people."

Shaking her head, she rolled her eyes, turning to pick up some dirty clothes lying about. She normally didn't care so much about tidiness, but she had to do something to keep from looking at him.

"Morons…" she muttered under her breath. Throwing the clothes into a hamper, she said to him, "I'd get the hell out of here as fast as I could, you know, if I were actually free to go."

"Some of them have left already. Most of them want to be vampire again. They need either Damen or me for that. Until we can get everyone sorted out, they'll be here."

"Are you really the only two vampires in the world now?"

"As far as I know, but if there were any other vampires who had severed their sire bond, there could be others. It's likely there are."

"So, that's why you and Damen didn't change."

"Well, yes, but my body was also temporarily dead, so I suspect I would have been unaffected either way. I owe Nicas everything. His essence revived me and forced me back from death."

"And Nicas is why you've forgotten about me?"

"I haven't forgotten about you. I just don't feel anything for you other than a thirst for your blood. I told you this already."

"Good to know I'm just a blood bag to you... Just like I always knew I would be back when I was chosen." She moved for her secret library. "I'm tired, so just leave me alone."

Cocking an eyebrow, he said, "You aren't sleeping in here?"

Stopping, she turned her head to speak over her shoulder. "I'd rather not. I can't stop you from sharing the room, but I don't have to sleep beside you, even though it's what I want to do more than anything in the world right now."

"Then sleep with me."

His words caused Sabine to turn and face him. "Sleep *with* you or sleep beside you?"

"Either..." He shrugged. "Both."

For a moment, she thought about it. She needed the comfort only her Remy could give her, but he'd said himself that he was gone. Could she look past what he'd become and pretend that he was still the man she fell for?

After all, he still looked the same. Maybe if he kept quiet, she could fool herself into believing it was him and nothing had changed. *Yeah, right. This is still Remy at his core. He isn't going to keep his mouth shut. I just wish what he had to say was something I wanted to hear.*

Not bothering to answer, she let herself into her library, the same one he'd had built just for her, after quickly changing into a nightgown in the closet. She slunk down into the reading chair he'd picked out for her, falling asleep listening to her stomach growl.

CHAPTER 3

Late the next afternoon, Sabine woke up. In those few split seconds before her brain really became in tune with reality, everything that had happened the day before was gone. For those few moments, she was blissfully unaware of what awaited her in the next room. The memories came crashing back within seconds, and if she hadn't been awkwardly lying in her chair, the force would have knocked her on her ass.

She dreaded coming face to face with him again, though he was the only person she desperately wanted to be with. Her arms wrapped around herself as best she could as warmth began to moisten her eyes again.

Standing up suddenly, determination took over. No more crying. She was done. What did it really help anyway? She spent the next few minutes psyching herself up, telling herself that she was strong, and that she would get through this. She worked herself up so much she almost wanted to fight. Not physically, of course, but she felt like really giving him a piece of her mind. And speaking of her mind, she suddenly realized she'd left her bracelet sitting on the bathroom counter after she'd cleaned herself up the evening before when she'd spent so much time sulking in the bathroom. Her feet had been in need of first aid, and she'd slipped off the bracelet to keep it from getting wet while she tended to them.

A moment of panic reared its ugly head. What if he took it? Could he even hear her thoughts? What exactly could he do with this newfound power?

Flinging the closet door open, she stopped dead in her tracks. There he was, sleeping peacefully in their bed—a painful reminder of the man she'd grown to love. Her heart sank clear to her feet.

He certainly looked like her Remy, and slept like her Remy, but he wasn't her Remy. Not by a long shot... What a cruel twist of fate destiny had played on her. She'd dreaded coming to Willow Creek Manor even before she was officially selected. It wasn't until she'd fallen in love with him that her future didn't seem so bleak. Now she found herself exactly where she'd always feared she'd end up; a prisoner of the vampire lord.

She couldn't help but think about how he'd whisked her away on a European trek just to show her a portion of the world before she came to the Manor to live. Her dream of visiting every country in Europe had come true, and she had him to thank for that. She thought of their time together nearly every day when she would absentmindedly toy with the Eiffel Tower necklace he'd given her on her twenty-first birthday. She'd taken it off and tossed it in her purse the night she was supposed to marry Bastian. It was too much to carry when it became unbearably heavy with memories she wanted so desperately to relive.

It was during their time together traveling that they'd both realized their love for one another, though neither would admit it until after they returned to Willow Creek. A few weeks of pure bliss was all they were allowed until Remy was taken from her. The last she'd seen of her Remy, he was dead on the floor of the ballroom where she'd left him when she fled.

This Remy that replaced him was entirely different from the man he'd proven he was. This version of him was cold and aloof, much like he'd been during her first encounters with him back when he terrified her. *He changed then; maybe he'll change now.*

Her fingers ached to touch him. Maybe if she touched him while his guard was down, he'd feel the spark they had the way she always felt it when he touched her. Maybe he'd remember how he felt about her. Maybe he'd remember how awesome it was when they came together physically and emotionally. Crawling into the bed beside him, she lay on her side facing him. She studied him while he slept, her lips desperately needing to be against his.

Her fingers reached out and touched a soft strand of his dark hair before moving on to his cheek. His skin cooled her hand as it moved over him. She pulled away, fearing she'd wake him, and he'd make some snide remark about her being in bed with him.

Just as she was about to get up, his eyes opened. Longing to see them brilliant and green, a coldness settled over her as the dark abysses they'd become peered at her.

"What were you doing?"

"Nothing. I was just leaving."

He sat up, gazing at her with an intensity that made her stomach flutter. "Tell me."

"I wanted to touch you." Her hand worked the end of her wavy hair, twirling it between her fingers. "I thought maybe if I touched you one more time, you'd feel it again... the love we have."

"Had..."

"Yeah... It was stupid. I need to get out of here," she said, standing suddenly.

"Where are you going?"

"I guess back to the library. It's not like I can go anywhere else."

"Where would you go if you could choose?"

"Home."

"Then go. I won't stop you... for now."

She whirled around to face him. "Home isn't there anymore. It's for sale, and they're gone. They never bothered to tell me where they went."

"Perhaps you could speak to Mary Mercy. Maybe she could help you locate them, though I don't know when you'd be able to visit them. At least you'd know where they are."

Yes, Mary! Maybe she can help me find them. Maybe she can help me find my Remy, too.

"I wouldn't count on that. I am what I am, and though remnants of him and the things you have fond memories of may linger, they're far below the surface. You'll never find him."

"I guess you can hear my thoughts. I was wondering."

He hesitated for just a moment before standing up. As he looked at her and quickly turned his gaze away, a flicker of something passed behind his eyes. "Yes, you forgot to put on your bracelet after you took it off last night. I found it on the counter in the bathroom." In an instant, he was in the bathroom and then before her. Taking her hand in his, he slid the bracelet Mary had given her to shield her thoughts onto her wrist. "There."

"Can you hear everyone now?"

He nodded. "If I forget to tune them out. I can even hear Damen. It..." His eyes softened just a little before looking away. He dragged his hand through his hair.

"It what?"

"Nothing."

She knew how much the thought of hearing what was going on in other peoples' heads bothered him. He'd told her he had no desire to listen in on anyone's thoughts.

"You can talk to me, Remy. Even if you feel like you can't talk to anyone about what you've gone through, I'm still here. I'm still me, and I know you better than anyone else."

"It drives me mad. It's so loud since I've been used to the quiet."

"It must be hard to adjust. I didn't think you would want me to keep my bracelet once you remembered I had it."

"One less voice to keep out of my head is a good thing."

"For what it's worth, I'm sorry."

"For what?"

"For everything you've been through. I can't imagine what it must be like to die and then come back completely changed."

His face softened for just a moment before he stiffened again.

"Whatever." Pulling on a pair of jeans he'd slung over the back of a chair, he left the room without another word.

* * *

Walking through the mansion brought stares and silence from the human guests. Their thoughts assaulted him before he could put up a wall in his mind to block them out. Most of them were the same... variations of if and when he would give them their immortality back and if he'd set the offerings free.

Remy walked out of the front door into the bright afternoon sun. For the first time in his immortal life, the dulling of his powers in the sunlight was barely noticeable.

Racing into the woods, he found a clearing and sent out his energy. Within a second, he touched Damen's mind and summoned him. A few seconds later, Damen stood before him.

"You rang?"

31

"What the bloody hell are we going to do with all of these people?"

Damen shrugged. "Turn them?"

"I don't want that many vampires always coming to me for shit I don't care about... and I don't want to be bothered to feel them all the time. You were enough to keep track of, and I didn't even really do a good job at that. That's why I never made any others."

"At least they all know what to expect. It's not like they'd all be brand-new baby vamps who don't know how to do anything. Maybe just change a couple of them and let them sort the rest out."

"That could work. You choose an amount acceptable to you, and I will choose a few. I'll instruct them to change the others, and we can be done with it."

Damen was keenly aware that Remy's eyes weren't nearly as dark as they'd been earlier. It was a subtle shift that only a vampire would recognize, but they were definitely lighter than they had been before. Whether or not it actually meant something, he didn't know.

"Listen, man, we need to talk," Damen said.

"About?"

Damen raised his eyebrow. "Everything."

"I don't have time to talk about everything, so how about you narrow the list?"

"Fine. Sabine... Why are you being such a dick to her?"

"I'm not being anything to her."

"After everything that happened in the last few weeks... You were willing to die if it meant she would be free of Bastian, and now you act like she isn't worth your time. I don't get it."

"It's really none of your concern."

"Maybe it isn't, but she's the first one I've ever seen you have a connection with like that. Is it worth it to throw that all away?"

"Shut your arse, Damen. I need Mary Mercy to come here. Go and make sure you bring her back. Use force if necessary."

"Oh, yeah, because force always works so well on a witch... I'll leave soon." Damen glared at his maker before turning away to disappear into the woods.

"Wait..."

Damen stopped. As he turned back, he noticed Remy's eyes lightening to a shade of green closer to his normal hue.

"What is it now, Your Highness?"

"There is something else I need to speak to you about. I don't really have anyone else I can discuss this with, and it needs to stay between us... at least for now anyway."

"Spit it out already."

Reaching deep within himself, he laced his words with power, compelling Damen to obey him. *"You will not tell anyone about this part of our conversation.* I can't have anyone questioning me more than they already do, and I'm not sure that I'm not simply losing my mind."

Damen's body instantly felt the influence of Remy's command. "I'll keep it to myself."

"Since I came back, I don't feel like myself."

"No, shit. Really?" Sarcasm coated Damen's words. "Couldn't have guessed that."

"I lapse in and out of consciousness at times, and when I awake, my actions play like a movie in front of my eyes. I see myself as if I'm recalling a memory, but it isn't. Right now, I know I want to take Sabine into my arms and never let her go, yet when she is in front of me, I can't seem to think about anything but her blood and how she smells. The feelings I have for her disappear and she becomes... a blood bag."

"That's pretty strange... It has to be a side effect of being dead. Maybe you didn't come back right."

"I think I've gone off my trolley completely."

"You have to let me help. If it weren't for the guidance and help you've given me over the years, I'd be dead by now. I know you think you screwed up as a maker, but you didn't. Let me return the favor by finding a way for you to feel normal again."

Remy nodded, reaching out to touch Damen's shoulder just before his body stiffened and the look on his face went cold. His eyes darkened and an evil grin spread across his lips. "You're so easy to fool. I really had you going, didn't I?"

"Yeah, you did." Damen left Remy standing in the clearing as he took off back toward the mansion.

"Tell no one," Remy said, sending his influence to Damen one more time.

CHAPTER 4

Creeping quietly down the stairs and through the short corridor to the dungeon, she expected to see Bastian just as bloodied and beaten as Remy had been when he was imprisoned in the same cell.

She laid eyes on a perfectly kempt human Bastian, albeit with a bad case of what looked like bed head. Her mouth dropped open as she watched him for a few seconds without him knowing she was there. *I cannot believe he didn't hurt him.*

She whispered "Revelar" to herself so that Bastian could see her. How strange it was to make herself visible for Bastian when he was the reason she'd placed the cloaking spell on the dungeon in the first place. It was the only way she could visit with Remy when he was first locked up, before she had permission to see him.

He sat with his back against the far wall with his hands crossed in his lap. "You have come to gloat?"

Sabine's skin prickled with a flash of fear. Seeing Bastian in such a vulnerable place was hard to wrap her mind around. Even in human form, his presence was graceful, yet commanding.

"No. I came for answers."

"I have none... but there is an answer I would very much like to have from you. Would life as my bride have been so bad? Was escaping me worth all the chaos it created?"

"I honestly don't know," she whispered. Was it worth it? Had she known Remy would end up like he was now, she would've tried harder to find another way. She begged him not to kill Nicas, and had resigned herself to the fact that if being Bastian's wife temporarily meant they could free Remy and get the hell out of Willow Creek eventually, then it was worth it. "I don't love you, Bastian. I would have never been truly happy."

"Do you think you could have grown to?" He stretched his legs out in front of him and crossed his feet.

"I don't know, but it doesn't matter now anyway, does it?"

"I suppose not."

"What's it like? Being human after all the time you spent as a vampire?"

"I ache... physically, emotionally, mentally... I feel as if I have a bruise on my neck from Remy's fingers squeezing my throat earlier, though I cannot tell for sure... It hurts. I am exhausted, thirsty, and hungry. I do not care for it."

"Maybe he'll turn you back."

"That would be a worse fate yet. I do not wish to be Remington's progeny. He would make eternity unbearable for the wrongs he believes I have committed against him, ignoring all the good I have done for him over the centuries. His actions have shown me that he is not the same vampire I grew to love as my own son."

"Maybe you shouldn't have treated him the way you did then. Ever think of that? What you did was despicable. You had no good reason for locking him up and stealing me away."

Bastian shrugged his shoulders and looked away. "What does it matter now, right?"

"You have no remorse for locking him up, do you?"

"No. He knew what he was doing when he chose to defy me, and he was punished accordingly. I only wish I had killed him when I had the chance."

"I bet you do," Remy said from somewhere behind Sabine. "Reveal yourself, Sabine."

She whispered, "*Revelar,*" and faced Remy. "What are you going to do to him?"

"Nothing he wouldn't do to me."

"This needs to stop now. Remy, don't hurt him. He's weak and helpless. You're above that." She glanced at Bastian, and for the first time ever, she saw fear on his face as he stood up slowly in the cell.

"Am I, really? You haven't the slightest clue of who or what I am, do you? I don't govern my life according to what you feel is right or wrong. I am pure-blooded vampire, Sabine."

"Yeah, so? You were a vampire before, and you're still a vampire now."

"He was, yes, but his blood was diluted like everyone else coming after Nicas."

"I don't want to hear this shit anymore. You really need to stop referring to yourself like that. It doesn't make it any easier for me, contrary to what you think. All this 'him' and 'he' bullshit. Get over yourself already."

Remy watched her walk heavy-footed down the corridor and up the stairs. Though he felt nothing for her at the moment, there was still something about her he found intriguing. *Probably just her blood that's pulling me in. Nothing more.*

Turning to Bastian, he said, "You have no desire to be my progeny?"

"No. What you have done is unforgivable."

"You seem to be confused here. You see, *I* am in charge now, not you. You have no authority over me, so why should I care whether or not you forgive me for what I've done?"

"Nicas would have never condoned what you did. He wanted to sleep for eternity, but he did not want any harm to come to his vampire children. Of course, he thought we would all die instead of our vampirism being expelled."

"Not true... He knew exactly what would happen. He only kept it hidden because he knew that the vampire who managed to kill him would absorb his essence and become the most powerful vampire of all."

"You are lying."

"I'm not. I can see the sex and raw power of the demoness who offered immortality and immeasurable abilities to aid in the plight to take over that tiny village in the Carpathian Mountains and expand its lands. I can smell her smoky perfume, taste her hot flesh, and feel her body inside and out… We fucked under the full moon on a sacred burial ground three thousand years ago. Feeding on her was pure heaven, or hell, as it may be the case. It was her blood that created our race and her blood that runs through me now."

"You are speaking nonsense, Remy. You could not possibly know the origins of our kind. You are just elaborating on the origin stories you have heard. Even I know it was not a demoness who changed him. It was a demon, and there was no fornicating involved."

"I assure you, she was not male, and there was plenty of it going on."

"I still do not believe you. Nicas never fully explained how he came to be even to me, and I was his favorite child. "

"You were, and you will be again."

"Again? What do you mean again?"

"I only meant that now that Nicas' essence has merged with my own, it will be like having him as your maker again. I've decided to turn a select few. Though you will be my favorite by far but for more entertaining reasons than you'd like to think about, I'm sure."

"There is something you must know now. Brendon is still here. I am assuming she told you all about him once I lifted the coercion he placed on her. He is locked in a cell in the main holding area. Do what you will with him, but he will die if you do nothing. A pity it would be for him to not receive the punishment he so deserved."

"Brendon? Brendon? Who was Brendon again?" Remy tapped his chin, searching his memories for the answer. "Ah, yes. The little shit who thought it a good idea to taunt him while he was locked up. Why didn't you take care of him yourself?"

"Because I knew at some point you and I would make amends, just like we always have, and I was keeping him so that you could take your revenge on him. I thought you deserved to be the one to take care of him."

"How generous of you to consider him while you were claiming Sabine as your own and leaving his body to rot down here. I *almost* believed that for a second. Are you sure you just hadn't gotten around to dealing with him yet and are looking for a way out of this mess now?"

Bastian looked away from Remy, swallowing hard.

"No matter. I will deal with him in time. See you soon." With a menacing smile plastered on his face, Remy backed away slowly before disappearing into the dark.

"See you soon, Nicas…" Bastian turned to sit down when a cold hand grasped his neck and flung him across the cell.

"I should've known you'd figure it out, my son."

Bastian, surrounded by a cloud of dust, coughed and tried desperately to inhale. After a few moments, he said, "How could I not? You practically spelled it out with the details you let slip. I did not buy that referring to yourself as 'him' just to ease her pain for a second, especially when you continued to do it even after she left. You are too arrogant not to be noticed. Is Remington still within you or have you banished him?"

"He is still in here." He tapped his long finger to his temple. "Strong one, that lad. He's not easily subdued. He manages to break through occasionally before I pull him back. I see why you chose to turn him. He certainly is a strong fighter. It's a pity I never met him in person before all of this, but no matter now. His body is quite remarkable. It suits me well since mine was destroyed when he snapped my neck."

"Why are you punishing me, my lord? I was only ever a faithful progeny to you."

"Yes, until you failed me by allowing Remington to get to me. I did not want to be disturbed, yet here I am. Though I suppose I might as well make the most of it now that I've been awakened."

"Why not just leave us in peace? You were not always this sadistic."

"You've only forgotten my true nature. Centuries have dulled your memories of the way we were. Do you not remember all the innocents we slaughtered or the wars I had a hand in starting for my own pleasure?"

"I have not forgotten, but I also remember the maker who took pity on me when I was dying. You are capable of being something more than evil."

"I am taking pity on you again. You will become my child again, whether you like it or not, but in the meantime," he knelt down, catching Bastian's gaze, "be sure not to mention this little conversation to anyone. Wouldn't want my secret getting out."

* * *

I'm so over this. Sabine quickly threw a couple of items into a small suitcase, grabbed her purse, and hightailed it out of there before Remy could return from the dungeon. *So what if he comes after me? Let him. I'll just run again until he locks me away.* Running felt like a natural solution to Sabine. This was the fourth time in almost as many years she'd tried to run away to escape her fate with Remy and Willow Creek Manor. Maybe this time, she'd be successful; though she had a feeling deep down that it would only be a matter of time before she was found. Still, she had to try.

The thought of him feeding on her, though exhilarating at one time, disgusted her now, and it was only a matter of time before it would happen. His teeth scraping against her flesh would be magnificent, and she knew she couldn't bear it. The euphoria would control her and bend her to its will. She had to get away before he had a chance.

Where she would go, she wasn't sure. She'd always felt like she had a home away from home with one of her two best friends. Unfortunately, Delia had moved to New York City, and her other best friend, Lana, hadn't returned any of her texts recently. Just another person who had disappeared without a trace from her life.

It didn't matter anyway because he knew of every place she'd go to hide and those would have been dead giveaways. She had no money to get completely out of town, but she could try to get as far away as possible. Finding his car parked in the circle driveway out front where she'd left it, she slid into the driver's seat and started the engine. On the road within seconds, she couldn't help but be drawn to her parent's house.

It was silly, of course, to go back there. She'd already fled The Manor once, and Gretchen had known exactly where to find her. Still, it was where she wanted to be, though she wished her family were there. As she approached her street, she continued to drive instead of turning toward her old neighborhood.

She drove to the small grocery store in town, where she ditched the car because of the tank being close to empty and began to walk. Her heart broke for everything that had happened in the last couple of days—Remy dying, finding her family gone, Remy coming back completely different...

Where could her parents and sister have gone? And where was Lana, for that matter? Why hadn't she responded to her? It wasn't like her family to just leave her after they'd been so adamant about making sure they could continue to see her. Bastian had agreed, so why did they leave?

Could something have happened to them? Maybe they were hurt or worse. What if they're dead from some freak accident, and no one bothered to tell me?

Cleary Park became visible just ahead of her on the right. It was as good a place as any to sit and contemplate where her life was headed. She'd done it many times in the past. Her stomach fluttered as she thought of the very first time she'd ever met Remy at that same park. If he chose to come and find her, this would be another easy guess for him.

Or would it? He didn't have near as fond a memory of the place as she did. Even though he'd been a royal dick to her that night, it was the first time her attraction to him had reared its head. She'd tried to dismiss him, but he made her feel things that were hard to ignore. This was also the place she escaped to as a teenager when she needed to get away from her parents, and that was certainly not something Remy would identify with. Maybe it was the perfect place to go for the time being.

Making her way quickly across the large field in the middle of the park, she hurried toward the amphitheater where concerts by local artists and the high school band were held on most weekends when the weather was warm. There was a little area beneath the stage that was used to house instrument cases, and it was just big enough for her to use for shelter, at least for the night. She knew it was there, and just how big it was, because she'd used it to make out with boys back in her high school days.

Scraping her knee on the concrete, she crawled into the cubby and turned so that her back was against the wall and she could see if anyone approached. If they weren't crawling around on the ground, they wouldn't be able to see her.

A burning sensation began to radiate across her kneecap as a small amount of blood oozed to the surface. Sabine fished around in her purse until she found a small bottle of water. Taking a capful, she poured it over her knee and blew on the abrasion to soothe it. At least she could get some of the dirt out of it and the blood washed away. Hopefully, the water would dilute the blood in the process. *That's all I need, some random vampire happening by, smelling my blood and finding me... Oh, wait, Remy and Damen are the only ones left. Okay, so I don't want Remy to find me because of a few drops of blood.*

Searching through the soft fabrics making up her clothes, she pulled out a hoodie, laying it on the ground so she would have something to sleep on. Fumbling around in her suitcase, she found a T-shirt and wadded it up. The ground was hard, but at least she could lay her head on something soft.

Sleep eluded her for what seemed like hours. She tossed and turned, trying to get just comfortable enough to drift off to sleep. At the point of giving up, she finally gave in to a restless night of dreams.

* * *

Running... Sabine found herself being chased through a thick forest. Who or what was chasing her remained a mystery. All she knew was that she was in danger and had to get away.

She reached a thicket of brush and crawled underneath, hoping to hide her presence. Heavy footsteps slowed, trampling dry leaves in its path.

Sabine peeked out from behind branches, trying to catch a glimpse of her pursuer. Black, leather boots covered feet that were attached to long, lean legs. Those legs, clothed in tight leather pants, led to a naked, muscular torso with strong arms. Her stomach dropped as her eyes rose to see the face of Remy searching for her.

His eyes were cold and black. He was stiff and calculating as only his eyes moved and he occasionally sniffed the air, trying to detect just where she was hiding.

"Come out. Now."

As if she weren't in control of herself, she began to crawl out from the brush. Screaming at herself to stop, her body continued forward. She stood and walked slowly to him. His outstretched hand, beckoning her forward

Just as her fingertips grazed his, another voice shouted, "Stop, Sabine! Don't. He isn't who you think he is."

She whirled around to face another Remy. Her Remy. His eyes, brilliant and green just like she'd remembered them, pleaded for her to come to him.

"Don't give up on me," he said.

As she ran to him, he faded just as she reached him.

* * *

Damen raced through the woods until he came to the edge of town. Emerging from the thick forest, he found himself in front of a car dealership that just so happened to also have a motorcycle for sale sitting out front. *It has been far too long since I've been on one of those.* His slow-beating heart sped up at the thought of racing down the road on the back of the black Harley.

As he strolled over to it, a portly man in a suit hurried out to intercept him.

"Is there something I can help you with today, sir?" he asked with the biggest, fakest smile plastered on his face.

"Give me the key to this bike." Damen knelt down, examining the curves of the bike and the shininess of the chrome accents.

"You want to take it for a test drive?"

Turning to the man, he caught him in his gaze. "No, I want the bike. You're going to get me the key now. You can send a bill to Willow Creek Manor. Address it to Damen Hughes."

"Sure thing, Mr. Hughes. We'll get you on the road shortly."

A little while later, Damen hit the open road on the bike. He'd be at Mary's in a little over an hour if he went the speed limit. Of course, he didn't intend to go that slow. Confident he could maneuver the bike in any traffic situation, he opened it up and sped toward his destination.

He pulled up to her house and parked the bike. Mary met him at the front door before he could knock or ring the bell.

"What the hell is going on, Damen? Sam sent me a message. She said you were on your way and that Remy needed me to come there. Last I heard, Remy was locked up and y'all were hoping to get him free in time to stop Bastian from taking Sabine."

"Well, that worked, but then the shit hit the fan. Can I please come in?"

"Get your ass in here." She stepped aside, allowing him access to her home.

He plopped down on the couch and sighed, though he had no need to breathe. It was mostly for dramatic effect.

"Remy killed Nicas and died. All the vampires, except me, thanks to your unbinding spell, turned human. Nicas' power or some shit like that revived him. Now Remy is some bad-ass vampire with more power than any of us and doesn't really act like himself... in a nutshell."

"Okay... So what does that have to do with me?" She picked up a glass of iced tea and brought it to her lips.

"I have no fucking clue. I was ordered to come and get you... and to use force if necessary."

Mary practically spit out the sip of tea she'd just taken. "Damn, boy, you're gonna make me choke to death. You really think you can take me anywhere by force?"

"No, I don't, but I'm not sure that Remy can't."

"That'll be the day."

"Seriously, Mary, he isn't the same. Please, come with me. I don't want to see you get hurt."

Mary stewed for a second before focusing her eyes on Damen. "If you think my ass is getting on that bike, you've got another thing coming."

* * *

Sabine's leg jerked as if she'd been kicked, startling her awake. Half expecting to wake up in the middle of the woods where her dream had left her, she was surprised to still be in the cubby under the stage.

"Wakey, wakey..." Remy sat across from her, leaning back on his hands with his legs stretched out in front of him.

"Well, I guess it didn't take long for you to find me."

"I could smell your blood in the air as soon as I found my car. I'm getting bored watching you sleep, so get your ass up and come on. I'm hungry."

The moment had finally come. The one she'd been dreading the most...

CHAPTER 5

She crawled quietly out of the cubby and stood before him. "Where's my suitcase?"

"I sent it back with my assistant."

"Your assistant?"

"Yes, Gretchen."

"Remy, she's like your sister. Why would you call her your assistant?"

"She isn't anymore, is she? She'll technically be my daughter later this evening, but I really have no feelings one way or the other about her. I'd just as soon turn her loose once she's changed so she can go out into the world and make more vampires."

I need to see Gretchen. I was sort of a bitch to her, and it's clear now that she's probably hurting, too. How could she not when the person who has been her brother for centuries is now regarding her as an assistant and nothing more?

His arms snaked around Sabine's back, pulling her close and raising her off her feet.

She tried to push away from him, but his arms only tightened around her. "What are you doing? I can walk. Put me down!"

A low noise, like a cross between a chuckle and a growl, emanated from his throat. He leapt into the air, startling Sabine. Wrapping her arms tightly around his neck, she stared in awe at the ground getting further and further away.

Just when she was sure that they would go falling to the earth below, his body tilted slightly forward as they glided quickly through the air.

"You never told me you could fly," she whispered.

"He... I mean, I couldn't before. Much more convenient than anything else, if you ask me. I can't imagine traveling long distances any other way."

Resting her chin on his shoulder, she wrapped her legs around his waist. It was true he wouldn't drop her. She had to believe that some part of him, deep down, would never do anything to hurt her, but still, she felt the need to cling to him when they were so high in the air.

She breathed in his scent and closed her eyes, wanting to lose herself to him. As much as she loved when he'd fed from her before, his power making every touch feel damn near like an orgasm, she couldn't stand the thought of it now. She'd be helpless to him for that few moments that he fed on her. Would she give in to him or would she be able to remain strong and stand her ground? She didn't want this Remy, and she was trying hard to convince herself of that.

Minutes later, they began to descend and landed with a soft thud in the circled driveway in front of Willow Creek Manor. He sat her down gently and held onto her for an uncomfortable couple of seconds. When she looked up into his eyes, something about them changed for just a moment before he let her go. They were still black, but they seemed somehow less intense for that split second.

"I'll be in to see you shortly," he said as he turned and walked away, leaving her there confused and alone.

* * *

Close to an hour later, he finally made it back to her. As he entered the room, he noticed Sabine curled into a ball on the bed, quietly resting. Her breath was soft and steady as he studied her, trying to figure out what to do with her.

Why can I not just be with her the way we used to be? Every time I think of her, my heart opens wide and longs to embrace her, yet when I am face to face, I feel nothing but confusion. The way she looks at me makes me feel at odds with myself, like there are two forces within fighting over whether or not to love her.

He sat beside her on the bed, his power reaching out to caress her body and mind. She rolled over, head tilting up to look at him through hooded eyes. He leaned over her, studying her neck and the throbbing artery just beneath the skin. His fangs descended as he anticipated the taste of her blood flowing over his tongue and down his throat.

Her breast began to heave as her breathing quickened, and her body warmed with the power he sent to her to numb any pain he might cause her. As he brushed a few strands of hair away from her neck, her body reacted to the graze of his fingertips. He lowered his head, softly licking at her flesh before plunging his teeth into her skin. The blood, hot and sweet, hit his mouth. Immediately, he pulled her to his chest, cradling her.

He sucked the life force from her body, replenishing his own and warming his skin as it flowed through him. Soft moans of pleasure escaped her lips as his cock hardened while he envisioned himself deep inside of her. Fangs disengaged from her skin. Pulling back, he peered down at the look of sheer pleasure plastered on her face, and it made him want her that much more.

Laying her back on the bed, he settled himself between her legs and buried his face in the crook of her neck, inhaling her scent. He pulled his power away from her to gauge her reaction. If she still wanted him, he planned to fuck her long and deep, but if she didn't…

"Shall I keep going?" he asked quietly in her ear. She pushed his shoulders up, lifting his head in the process, and gazed into his eyes, searching for something—what, he didn't know—before she looked away. In that moment, he wanted to scream that he loved her, but something held him back. A force within kept him at bay.

"I don't know."

"It's a simple yes or no."

"No, it isn't."

"It is. Would you like me to pleasure you or not?"

"More than anything." Her voice squeaked, breath catching in her throat.

"Then what's the problem?"

"You."

"Me?" He sighed and rolled off her. "I can see this is never going to work for either of us." The words fell from his mouth, but they didn't taste like his own.

"Remy... I just need some time to figure out how I feel about everything. I know I loved who you were, but I don't know you anymore, and I'm scared." The dream she'd had played games with her mind. She was still drawn to him, no matter how hard she tried not to be, but was she willing to give up the man she'd fallen in love with in exchange for the one in front of her?

"I won't hurt you."

"Maybe you won't hurt my body, but you *will* hurt me because you don't care about me anymore. I'm nothing more than a warm body and a meal for you now. What happens when you get tired of me?"

"I don't see myself ever tiring of your blood, but you'll be free if it does happen. Isn't that what you've always wanted?"

"It's more complicated than that, and you know it. I love you. I want to be at your side no matter where in the world that may be, but I can't do it if I'm terrified that you'll throw me away at any second."

"How can I help ease your mind of these things?"

"Love me again... Or help me find my family so I at least have them to go home to."

Yes, that was the answer. He'd simply love her again, though he didn't feel as if he had stopped. "I will try, though I can't promise anything."

"Try to love me or try to find my family?"

The corner of his lip turned up before he spoke again. "I'll try…"

CHAPTER 6

Mary Mercy, driving a hunter green Jeep, followed Damen on his Harley up the winding road to Willow Creek Manor. She eyed the place cautiously as she parked and got out.

Damen smiled and turned toward her. "Welcome to Willow Creek, Mary."

"Yeah, I have a feeling I'm going to want to crawl out of my skin to get away from this place before it's over with."

"You and me both, sister."

Mary rolled her eyes at Damen before walking through the front door and into a house full of people. As she glanced around at some familiar and some not-so-familiar faces, she saw people who she'd known as vampires for years, now weak and helpless as they tried to adjust to mortal lives.

"Where is he?"

"I don't know for sure, but we can check his and Sabine's room."

"How is she?"

He shrugged and motioned with his head for Mary to follow. A few moments later, Damen knocked on the door of the bedroom and waited for an answer. Sabine cracked open the door slowly, trying to sneak a peek at who might be on the other side. Her eyes met Mary's, and she flung open the door. Her arms shot out, embracing her and pulling her closer.

"I missed you, too, girl," Mary said, returning Sabine's hug.

"I'm so happy to see you!"

"Me, too, sweetheart. Is Sam with you?"

Sabine shook her head. "No. Sam's been missing in action since the other night."

Mary's eyebrows raised as her mouth started to hang open. "*What*?"

"Oh, God, no!" Sabine waved her hands wildly. "Nothing's wrong! I'm sorry. I shouldn't have said it like that. I introduced her to her mother and she's been with her ever since."

"I knew her mother wasn't dead. Just had a feeling all along."

"Come in here. No sense in standing out in the hallway."

"Where's Remy?"

Sabine stiffened. "I don't know. He left a while ago. He never really tells me what he's doing and, honestly, I don't care to know what he's doing either. What brings you here anyway?"

"He sent this one," she said, motioning her thumb in Damen's direction, "to bring me back."

"And, no, I don't know why. I've already told Mary the extent of what I know," Damen said, plopping

58

himself down on the edge of the bed. "For once, I wish I could read his mind."

The door whooshed open as Remy appeared in front of them. "You don't have to long for listening to my private thoughts because I'm going to tell you what's going on. First and foremost, I need the cloaking spell placed on the library and the dungeon dismantled."

"Hell to the no... I taught that girl the spell to help protect her, at your request I might add, and I'm not taking it down now."

Remy's mouth hardened into a straight line. His eyes fixed on Mary. "Do it."

"I'm not scared of you. You know that, right?"

In a flash, Remy had Mary backed against the wall before she had time to stop him. She threw her hand up and whispered something in Latin. Remy cocked his head to the side. "Oh... Yeah, that won't work. So I suggest you do as I say."

"What the hell happened to you?"

"This again..." he said, sighing. "I'm going to have to make some sort of sign and carry it around so I don't have to repeat this for eternity. I died. I came back stronger than ever, and I don't give a shit about anything or anyone."

Sabine let out a small breath as she looked away.

"Tell me something." Mary looked straight into his eyes and didn't back down.

"What?"

"Why do you want the cloaking spell taken down?"

His jaw clenched as he glanced at Sabine over the arm he used to hold Mary in place. "Because she hides from me, and I don't like it."

"So, you'd rather her not have a place to be safe from other threats because she wants to ignore you from time to time? I don't blame her for wanting to get away from you." Mary scooted against the wall to the side and away from Remy. "Which way are the rooms you want me to de-spell?"

"Through the closet and through the secret door by the fireplace."

Mary strutted over to the closet door and through to the back where she found the library. She went quiet for close to five minutes as she meditated, whispering inaudible incantations to herself. Finally opening her eyes, she said, "This one's done. Show me the other door."

After the dungeon was magic-free, Remy asked to speak with her alone. The others left, but not without hesitation.

"There is another reason I have summoned you here. I need a witch by my side."

"I'm not moving here. Forget it."

"I wouldn't dream of asking you to. I want you to be Sabine's mentor."

"Does she know what you have planned for her?"

"No, but I'm sure she'll agree. As I look back through my memories with her, I see that she very much enjoyed casting that cloaking spell, and she always seemed so intrigued by witches whenever he would speak of them."

"Who?"

Remy crinkled his brows. "What?"

"Who? Who is 'he'? You said when he spoke to her about witches."

"Simple slip of the tongue. I was referring to myself as 'he' when I spoke to her about the vampire I was before I died. I thought it would make her get over him, or me, faster if she could see me as altogether different."

"Uh-huh... Because that was really going to work... I'll train her, but I won't do it here. I need to be on my own home turf with my own stuff so I'm not on edge all the time and can really focus on showing her the way."

"Fine, but you must stay here a little longer before you take her. I have another task for you to perform."

CHAPTER 7

Everyone gathered in the ballroom, waiting for him to make his grand entrance. Like a shimmer of light, he materialized out of nowhere. Sabine wondered to herself why he would teleport when it normally drained him of energy. *Guess it's not a big deal anymore now that he's Super Vampire.*

"The time has come for some of you to become vampire once more. The overwhelming majority of you will not be turned by me. My prodigy, Damen, has suggested I turn a select few of you. After that, those vampires may go on to turn others as they see fit. Damen will be changing some of you as well. Those of you whom I am gifting immortality to may now step forward. They know who they are already, so don't try to sneak into the group if you aren't one of them."

A few faces in the crowd began to make their way forward. The only one Sabine recognized was Gretchen. She reached out, squeezing Gretchen's hand as she passed. She flashed an indifferent smile at her in return. *Guess I sort of deserved that one.*

"Those who Damen has notified may also step forward."

More bodies moved toward the center of the room. All in all, there were around twenty people gathered in front of the two vampires.

"Someone must go fetch Bastian from his cell. Who will volunteer?"

"I will." Sabine stepped forward, raising her hand.

Rage flashed on Remy's face. "You will not. He could easily overpower you. He may not be a vampire now, but he is still a man who happens to be bigger than you."

"I'll go with her," Sam said. "He won't get anything over on me," she said confidently. "I'll shift into a tiger and swat his ass if he tries anything."

Remy nodded in Sam's direction with a hint of a smile on his face. "Fine. Go, now. I want him here before we begin."

The two left the ballroom and headed back to Sabine's room. In an effort to kill the quietness, she decided to chitchat with her friend.

"How are you and your mom getting along?"

"Couldn't be better. Thank you so much for bringing us back together. I can't believe I have my mother back."

"I'm happy for you." Sabine couldn't help but think about her own mother and wonder what she was doing and where she was.

"For the entire first night, we just tried to get to know each other. I've dreamt of talking to my mother for as long as I can remember. It was amazing."

"I bet it was." Sabine smiled warmly at Sam.

"Oh, shit... Here I am talking about how happy I am with my mom when I know you're worried sick about yours and your family."

"Don't do that." Sabine stopped and put her hand on Sam's shoulder. "Don't ruin your happiness with my issues. Promise me."

"Alright, I promise."

They continued to walk, making it back to the room quickly. Sabine made her way to the fireplace and pushed the stone that made the secret door open. As she walked quickly down the stairs, she noticed the dungeon seemed colder than usual and smelled faintly of something acrid.

They stepped into view of the cell, only to find it completely empty.

"What the actual fuck? Where did he go?" Sabine searched around in the dark. "Bastian?" she yelled.

"It looks like he just disappeared. Look," Sam said, pointing to the cell door. "It's still closed and locked. He just vanished."

"Remy is going to have a shit fit over this one. How is this even possible?"

"Was he still a vampire? Maybe we just didn't realize it. He could've poofed his way out of here."

"No, he was definitely human... I think, anyway. He said he didn't like being human and went into detail about how he felt."

"Yeah, well, he's also a liar."

"True. We better go tell Remy."

"I'll let you go first." Sam stayed put and waited for Sabine to go ahead of her.

"Gee, thanks!" Hand landing on her hip, Sabine let out a short chuckle.

"What? He'll be less likely to kill the messenger if *you're* the messenger."

"I wouldn't be too sure of that one anymore." Sabine headed up the stairs and back to the ballroom with Sam following close behind.

She cautiously opened the doors and stepped through. Remy's gaze landed on her. In an instant, he was before her.

His face became stern and unmoving, save for the slight curling of his lip.

"Where is he?" he asked through clenched teeth.

"Gone," Sabine said quietly, shifting her weight.

Remy grabbed both Sabine and Sam around the waists and teleported to the dungeon.

"What the hell did you do that for?" Sabine yelled as she yanked herself away from his grasp, becoming dizzy in the process. She looked over at Sam, who braced herself against the wall. Teleportation was an awesome thing to witness, but it wasn't all that fun to experience as a human. It made Sabine feel like her head was on backwards and her stomach was tied in knots when she didn't have time to close her eyes first.

Remy surveyed the cell and the floor. "Did you have any part in this?"

"Absolutely not!" Sabine said as she crossed her arms.

"Sam?"

"Hell no!"

"There aren't any fresh footsteps outside of the cell, except for yours, but there are two sets inside."

"How is that possible? Did someone teleport in there?" Sam asked.

"More than likely."

"You and Damon are the only ones who can do that, aren't you?" asked Sabine.

"No. Some witches can do it as well. Go get Mary. Now!"

"No need. I'm right here."

Remy was so entranced by the situation that he failed to notice Mary and Damen at the foot of the stairs walking toward them.

"Did you do this?"

"No, but I'd know that scent anywhere. Do you smell it?"

"Of course I smell it. It's eerily familiar, yet I can't place it."

"Most of the time, the scent of magic is undetectable, except for those times when a witch expels large amounts of it. It's my mother's magic." Mary's mother, Kristine, had died placing the spell on Nicas that kept him subdued over the centuries. Though she was already dead, she had crafted the spell responsible for making the town residents forget about vampires once they left Willow

Creek. She'd left it for one of her students to perform. "She loved that bastard so much that she left me behind without thinking twice about it. No doubt she's done whatever she could now to save him."

"When Sara Crowley was haunting me, she mentioned that your mother had enchanted her so she wasn't able to tell us what was hidden here. She was already dead when she did that, so I guess it makes sense that she could still use magic even now."

"That still doesn't explain the extra set of footprints. Ghosts don't leave them behind. Damen, try to figure out if any of our guests have left abruptly."

Damon nodded. "I'll ask around. I can't remember all the people who have been here since this all began, but someone might have noticed something suspicious."

Sam spoke up. "Maybe Sara could help you again."

Sabine shook her head. "She's gone. I haven't seen or heard from her since before Remy killed Nicas. Taking Bastian down was her only concern. Once that happened, she was just gone."

Remy waved his hand nonchalantly. "He is human now. He is no threat to me. I'll find him sooner or later, and he'll regret it when I do. Come…" he said as he turned to leave. "I have business upstairs to attend to." He touched the small of Sabine's back to guide her up the stairs.

She stood firm. "I'm going to bed. I have no desire to see a bunch of people turned into vampires," Sabine said.

His jaw clenched as his hand dropped to his side. "Fine with me. You can be good and rested for my next feeding."

"Can't wait," she muttered as she walked up the stairs.

CHAPTER 8

Remy sunk his teeth into the flesh of eight different people. He drained them of half their blood and had them feed from him as he passed some of his power to them, willing them to become vampires. The process was very easy, if not boring, for the standard maker/progeny relationship. However, there was another way to turn someone. Very few vampires ever employed the method, though it was more entertaining, if not mind blowing altogether. The concept of creating a mate was not one most vampires embraced though, and the process was rarely used.

After Damen turned his chosen lot, Remy summoned Mary forward.

"You performed an unbinding spell on me, yes?"

"Uh-huh."

"Do it for my new progenies as well. They've all been vampire before and don't need me to teach them the way. I'd rather cut them loose than to have to deal with them for another second."

Gretchen stepped forward. "Even me, my brother? I will be weak and may still need your protection."

"Especially you. I'm not your brother anymore, and I don't need a reminder of what I used to be."

Gretchen clutched her chest and hung her head. Glancing at Mary out of the corner of her eye, she whispered, "Unbind me first."

"I haven't found out anything yet, and now people are starting to leave. I don't know how I'm going to be able to track down some mysterious person who vanished into thin air." Damen paced back and forth across the large room.

"Keep looking. Someone has to have seen or heard something suspicious. Have you checked the other dungeons?"

He stopped, looking down at the floor. "No. I didn't even think about it."

Remy threw his hands into the air. "Must I do everything myself?"

"Yeah, maybe you should." Damen's eyes darkened as he glared at Remy. "Frankly, I'm getting tired of your bullshit already."

"I will go look. In the meantime, I suggest you leave. I've had enough of your bullshit as well."

Moments later, Remy stood before a row of cells, four on each side. There were only two prisoners being held there at the time. One was a former vampire who had crossed over the Willow Creek border without Bastian's permission. Remy had been told she was being held for questioning, though that didn't matter to him at all. He couldn't care less about who came and went through the town or their reasoning for doing so.

He came to the pitiful creature in her cell, her blonde hair darkened by dirt and her face sunken in from malnutrition. She had been far older than any of them could know, and he remembered her from years back. It was a mystery to him how Bastian was able to capture her in the first place. But then he remembered that Bastian had been drawing his power magically and was stronger than most vampires. She'd been stunning as a vampire, but was now sickly and weak as a human.

Feeling a pang of sympathy for the woman, he opened her cell door. Bending his head to her, he drained her of most of the blood she had left.

Biting his wrist, he held it to her mouth. "Drink, my child."

Her lips weakly covered the rapidly healing wound and took his blood into her mouth. His power washed over her, mingling their blood. Within seconds, her skin and eyes brightened. "Go upstairs to Mary so the unbinding spell can be completed."

"Thank you," she said and left.

He moved further down the corridor to the cell that housed the other prisoner—Brendon. He was going to take joy from torturing this one. Brendon had been allowed to feed on Sabine, and because he was a sick and twisted former offering, he took great pleasure in hurting her. He didn't even allow her to scream from the pain. *He will pay for what he did to her.* As soon as the thought entered his mind, he stopped in his tracks. *Why do I keep doing this? I love her, so why is it so difficult to show her that I still do?*

He growled loudly as the empty cell came into view and the same acrid scent hit his nose. "Bloody hell!"

Searching for more evidence, he noticed only one set of footprints inside the cell this time, instead of the two he'd seen in Bastian's cell. *Kristine must have taken control of Brendon's body, but why wouldn't she just take over Bastian's body instead? Unless she wanted to be able to communicate with him. She used this one because his absence wouldn't have been noticed right away. Clever little witch...*

Speaking of clever little witches. I've got my own to attend to.

* * *

"Sabine?" He sat down next to her and gently touched her shoulder. "Wake up."

"Bite me... Oh, yeah, I forgot. That's what you're planning to do, right?"

"Soon, but I have something to discuss with you."

"What?"

"I'm sending you to live with Mary for a while."

She sat up, searching his eyes for any sign of deceit. "Why would you do that?"

"I want her to teach you magic. She's the best witch for the job, and I need you to learn."

"So you're sending me away? So much for trying..."

"There are more important things to worry about at the moment than whether or not we'll be lovers again. I need a witch, and I want you to be the one."

"How long will I be gone?"

He shrugged. "However long it takes. That really depends on you and how willing you are to learn."

"Mary said it took years and years to master witchcraft and magic. You're letting me go for that long?"

"If necessary."

"When do I leave?"

"In the morning, but I need to feed from you first."

"How will you ever live without my blood?" she asked with a hint of sarcasm to her tone.

"I won't have to because I'll personally be checking in on your progress as I see fit. I'll feed then."

"Let's get this over with." She tilted her head, exposing her neck to him. Warmth spread over her, and her skin began to tingle. At her core, desire rose as he leaned forward.

Remy moved closer to her. The sound of her heart thumped in his ears. In that moment, the love and passion he had for her fully returned. He fought desperately to cling to it as he kissed her neck instead of drinking from her. He strained to tell her how he felt, but every time he opened his mouth, the words wouldn't come out.

Despite his efforts, the love fell from his grasp while hunger set in, blocking out everything except for satiating himself. He bit down hard on her skin, his teeth puncturing the artery as her blood flowed down his throat.

Managing to move her arm, she reached up to run her fingers through his hair. She knew it was the power he had over her, but there was nothing more she wanted in that moment than to give her body to him. It didn't matter that he didn't act like the man she fell in love with because he was *still* Remy.

Pulling his fangs out of her, he licked at his lips so as to not spill any of her precious blood. He quickly healed the two tiny puncture wounds. His power followed him away from her as he sat up, preparing to leave.

"Wait," she said with barely a breath. "I need something from you before you send me away." Sabine sat up on her knees facing him. Touching his shoulder, she gently pushed at the neck of his shirt, exposing his collarbone. She inhaled sharply as her fingers grazed his skin, warm from her blood coursing through his body.

"I've told you I still want your body," he said in a husky tone, placing his hand over hers.

"I know," she said, briefly looking away before meeting his gaze once more, "but I need something else."

"And what would that be?" he asked, finger grazing her jawline.

"Lie to me," she whispered.

He leaned in and kissed her hard on the lips. It wasn't at all like the passionate, love-filled kiss she remembered. It was cold and primal.

Pulling herself away from him, she said, "You don't understand. Pretend like you still love me... like you still care."

He studied her intently with a look on his face somewhere between laughing hysterically and giving into her wish. Just when she thought it best to tell him never mind and that she'd made a mistake, he reached out and lightly gripped her side. His touch sent chills up her spine.

Pulling her closer to him, he kissed the curve of her jawline ever so softly before nibbling at her ear. His cool breath grazed her flesh as he whispered, "No need to lie. I love you still."

A single tear slid down her cheek. His tongue caught it before it could fall from her face. When she pulled back to look at his beautiful face, brilliant green emeralds returned her gaze.

"Remy! Your eyes…"

"Shhh… Lay back, love."

The term of endearment didn't go unnoticed. It was the first time since he'd come back from the dead that he'd called her that. Her breath caught in her throat as the word "love" flowed passed his lips. She hadn't realized just how much she'd missed it until the moment he said it.

His body, heavy against hers as he kissed the hollow of her throat, felt familiar. He worshipped her body, taking his time undressing her and himself as he paid special attention to the most sensitive of areas before positioning himself between her legs.

"You're sure this is what you want, love?"

She bit at her lip as she nodded, urging him to keep going. Once he was inside her, all her thoughts and fears of the unknown with him disappeared. The connection they had was still there. She could feel it, even if he tried to deny it before.

Her mind was made up. Giving up on him wasn't an option. If her Remy could appear now, he could be there with her all the time. Maybe all it would take was some sort of spell to harness his power so it didn't command him. He'd told her himself that power like that could drive a vampire mad. Since she was to learn magic anyway, she would find it for him and make him be what he was once again. She would save him.

Her hips rose to meet his as he thrust into her. Clearing her mind, she let herself relax and enjoy him—his body, his scent, the taste of his lips. Her body clenched, sending an orgasm rocketing through her body as she screamed out his name.

She'd finally gotten what she'd been looking for all this time—her Remy.

CHAPTER 9

Awakening in his arms was a dream come true. Her head lay on his chest as the faint beat of a heart thumped occasionally. A smile danced across her face as something from the other side of the room caught her attention.

It only took her eyes a second to focus before seeing Remy standing in the corner of the room with chains binding him. Manacles attached to thick chains placed on either wrist restrained him from reaching out to her. Her brows crinkled, mouth slightly agape, as she sat up, looking back and forth between the two identical vampires.

Lightly placing her feet on the floor, she walked over to her chained lover as she glanced at the sleeping Remy on the bed. She touched his face. His flesh was cold and sallow.

He blinked heavily and licked at his cracked lips. The chains clinked as he struggled to move toward her. "Don't trust him. He isn't me." His voice was thin and raspy.

"What do y—"

She was yanked from sleep abruptly as Remy pushed her arm off him and got out of bed. He walked across the room, reaching for the bathroom door.

"Come back to bed one more time before I go. I'm going to miss you." She allowed herself a moment of weakness with him because she knew it was only a matter of time before she could figure this all out.

He turned and glared at her with eyes even darker than they'd been before. "I'll see you in a few days. Perhaps we can reconnect then."

"What's happened? Your eyes were normal last night... even after."

"You told me to lie to you, so I did." He walked into the bathroom, shutting the door behind him.

How could I be so stupid? It was all an act. Exactly what I asked for. She could hear the faint sound of water running in the shower as she sunk back down into the covers. *I'm never leaving this bed. I'd rather die than face another day outside of these blankets.*

* * *

"Get up, girl. We've got shit to do today." Mary flipped the covers off Sabine, only for her to flip them back over her head.

"I don't want to." She pulled the covers into a cocoon, shielding herself from the light.

"I know it, but you have to. I don't know what'll happen if we don't get this started soon. You need to get your stuff packed if you haven't already, but I've got an exercise for you to do before we go."

"I don't have anything packed. I hate packing. I'm a master procrastinator and have mastered the art of packing at the last minute."

Mary chuckled. "Well, come on already. I'm going to teach you how to clear your mind today. I think that trick just might come in handy. I guess you can pack when we're done."

Reluctantly, Sabine got out of bed and made herself somewhat presentable. If throwing her hair in a wet, messy bun after getting a quick shower, and slipping into some yoga pants and a tank top was considered presentable.

Within the hour, Sabine followed Mary down a path into the woods. The sound of birds echoed through the trees as the breeze blew around them. The slight buzzing of insects caused Sabine's skin to crawl. She was never a fan of bugs, and they tended to creep her out. If she could just manage to get out of there without seeing a snake, well then, maybe the day wouldn't end up being quite so shitty.

"This'll do," Mary said, spreading a purple blanket out onto the ground. "Sit."

Sabine did as she was told. She sat with her legs crossed and leaned on one knee. "Now what? I close my eyes and block everything out?"

"You've got it. It's a little harder to do than you might think. The reason I want you to learn this now is because once you start doing more complex magic, you'll need to have mastered this skill. It's the state of mind you will always need to begin with when using the magic within. Plus, it helps to clear your mind when you're going through stressful shit. The sooner you can do it, the better for your mental state."

"Do I just begin?"

"Yeah, just close your eyes and try to visualize yourself in a place with no noise… no buzzing, no chirping, no nothing… just silence."

She closed her eyes and tilted her head to the side. "Can I lay down or do I have to stay sitting up?"

"It's up to you, but if you lay down, you're probably going to fall asleep, and that's taking it a little too far. Now, take a deep breath and let it out. Continue to breathe in and out deeply as you focus on silence."

She envisioned herself in a white room, sitting in a comfortable chair. Try as she might, the chirping of birds kept ripping through her silence. The skin on her arm began to itch. Trying hard to ignore it, she finally had enough. "I can't do this," Sabine said, scratching at her arm. "How in the hell am I supposed to block everything out if something random like an itch is going to snap me right out of it?"

"It takes time and patience. You'll eventually get to the point where someone touching you won't bring you out of it if you don't want to be bothered."

"That can't come soon enough."

"You can practice more in the Jeep on the way back to my house."

"Is Sam coming with us?"

"I'm not sure yet. I think she's probably going to go wherever her mom goes, and I don't think Remy has officially released her or the others yet."

"I hope he does soon. I realize I'll probably never be free of it all, but maybe the others can be."

"You're going to make an excellent witch, you know that?"

"What do you mean?"

"I can see how much you care about others. I just have a feeling whatever magic you master, you'll use for good."

"Let's just hope 'good' is what he has in store for me, though I'm not counting on it."

"All the more reason for you to get as strong as you can as fast as you can, so maybe you won't always have to do things you don't want to do."

Sabine stared off into the distance for a few minutes before speaking. "I need to tell him goodbye."

"We'll have time before we leave."

"No, I mean tell him goodbye for good. He isn't the person I knew, and no matter how much I want him to try to be, he isn't. I have to let him go." It was the last thing she ever wanted to admit to herself, but in her heart, she knew it was what she had to do. The connection from the night before that she thought she felt was nothing but a lie. It never would've happened had she not asked him to lie to her in the first place. She still couldn't believe she'd fallen or it so easily.

"He really isn't acting anything like himself, is he?"

"Not one bit."

"It's the power. Drives them all mad when they get a taste of it, and he seems to have hit the jackpot."

"He told me that once, but I guess I didn't fully understand it at the time," Sabine said, shaking her head. "I do now…"

"Tell ya what, when we get back to my house later, we'll crack us open a bottle of wine or two or three, I'll bake you something chocolaty and decadent, and we'll have a good old-fashioned, girly mope fest. Then we'll start magic learning tomorrow. Sound good?"

Sabine nodded and reached out to Mary for a hug.

They headed back to the Manor shortly after so that Sabine could get ready to leave for an indefinite amount of time. Her nerves worked against her, and every time she stopped for more than a second, she became nauseated and her hands shook. Whether it was leaving the Manor, saying goodbye to Remy, or just the overwhelming doom she felt in regard to her life and the loss of her family, she wasn't sure. They were all equally nerve-racking in their own ways.

I'm going to focus on them instead of all the other bullshit going on. Remy is gone. I know that now, and I need to focus on getting my family back. Maybe Mary can teach me a location spell so I at least know where they are. But just then, a thought hit her with such force that it almost knocked her off her feet. *What if they don't want me anymore either?* She shook the thought away as quickly as it'd come. There was no reason to believe her family didn't want anything to do with her. There had to be some other explanation for their sudden disappearance than that one.

As she perused her belongings, trying to decide what to take, she came across the jewelry box sitting on top of one of the chest of drawers in the room. When she pulled on the handle, the door opened. She'd only meant to put the necklace with the Eiffel Tower pendant Remy had bought her for her birthday back into it. If she were saying goodbye to him, she had to go full force or she'd never get over him, and she didn't need a constant reminder of the wonderful time they'd had in Europe.

As the door opened, she gasped. There, hanging from one of the tiny hooks, was the necklace that belonged to Remy's mother, the one he'd killed another vampire over just to get it back. He kept it on him almost all the time. In fact, if he had clothes on at all, the necklace was always tucked into a pocket or around his neck, hidden just underneath his shirt. He'd vowed never to lose it again. It wasn't something he took lightly.

Her fingers reached out, gently grazing the purple stone. *He'd never leave this behind for anything.*

"You can have that if you like it." She'd been so entranced with the necklace that she hadn't noticed him entering the room.

"You've never offered it to me before. Why would you now?" She eyed him curiously.

"It's nothing to me. Just a cheap piece of clutter really, but you seem to like it."

"This was your mother's... your wife's..."

Remy shrugged his shoulders

"You know what? I think I will take it." *If he doesn't care about it anymore, at least I can. He doesn't deserve to have it if he wants to throw it away.*

Undoing the clasp, she fumbled with putting the necklace on herself. His cool fingers took the chain from her and placed it around her neck. She quickly tucked it down into her shirt and turned to him.

"I guess this is goodbye."

"I will see you in a few days. I see no need for goodbyes."

"No, I'm saying goodbye to the Remy I knew. I know I can't ever get away from you completely since you're having me trained to be your magical lackey, but this time away with Mary will be a Godsend. I can't stand to look at your face while I mourn the man I love. Feed on someone else and leave me be... Please?"

His eyes grew intense and for a split second, she feared he would hurt her.

His hands fisted at his sides as he glowered at her. "I'll feed from only you." Grabbing her face on either side, he kissed her deeply, claiming her with his lips.

Her body relaxed into his arms, commanding her mind to give in. Why did he have to taste so much like she remembered? As her arms instinctively wrapped around him, she pressed herself against his body. Her heart raced as if it could beat out of her chest at any moment. Could she ever truly make herself let go?

Pulling his lips away from hers, he stepped back. His eyes were bright and green. Just as she noticed the change, he looked away, closing his eyes as he shook his head. When he looked back, dark pits peered back at her. He leaned in once again as if he were going to kiss her.

At the moment his lips should have crashed into hers, he caught her gaze, lulling her into a light trance, and said, "Don't try to run away from Mary's. You won't go far without my permission." When he looked away, the trance was lifted.

Her hand jolted out and smacked him hard on the cheek. His flesh reddened for a split second before returning to its normal pale hue. Jaw clenching, he stared at her with his mouth set into a straight, hard line.

"How dare you use coercion on me?"

"You have a history of running, and I can't have you doing that. I need you to focus because I need a witch. The sooner, the better."

"Why did you kiss me? What the hell are you trying to prove?"

"I have nothing to prove. I like kissing you, and it seemed like the best thing to do to lighten the mood. Your lips are soft and have a taste that is all too familiar to me. Truth be told, I rather enjoyed our time together last night. I do believe it was you who wanted me to try to love you again. That's what I'm doing."

"Don't bother." Pulling the handle up on her suitcase, she began to wheel it behind her as she walked heavy-footed to the door. Just as she turned the doorknob and pulled it open, she turned back to see him one last time, though she knew she shouldn't.

Sneering, he took a step toward her.

"I fucking hate you," she said, slamming the door behind her as she left.

CHAPTER 10

The cork gave way with a loud pop. "This Amish wine has a pretty good kick to it. Should do the trick in no time," Mary said, handing Sabine a glass of peachy alcoholic goodness.

"I'm not much of a drinker, so I'm guessing I'll feel it shortly."

"I ordered us a pizza with extra cheese. They also have a to-die-for hunk of chocolate cake, so I figured I'd just buy us each one. No use in waiting all evening for me to bake something."

"Sounds glorious... Can I ask you something?"

"Sure."

"Am I doing the right thing? By letting him go, I mean...?" She searched her mind for the words she needed to express the confusion she felt, but none of them felt adequate.

"Honey, I can't give you the answer to that. That's something you have to figure out on your own, but I will say, if he isn't the same person you fell in love with, then I think you made the right choice."

"That's the weird thing. He acts a lot more now like he did when I first met him. Like he couldn't care less, you know? I hate to admit it, but that's when I started having a thing for him. I don't know if it was the whole bad boy, forbidden fruit thing he had going on, or if I'm just a giant weirdo."

"We're all a little weird sometimes. It's what makes us unique."

Sabine flashed a weak smile in Mary's direction. "Even though he does have that attitude, he's just not himself."

"Believe me, the attitude he has is typical for vampires who don't want a connection with anyone. It's common among them. That's also why most of them don't have other supes for friends or even acquaintances. There's always been folklore about vamps and witches or vamps and shifters not getting along because of some hatred that runs deep between the species, but it's really because most of them are just dicks."

"Yeah, and Remy is their king!" Sabine laughed hard at herself until her eyes began to mist over. Careful not to spill her wine, she sat the glass down on the coffee table so she could really enjoy the moment.

"Oh, honey, you got that right!"

Mary joined in the hysterics with a loud cackle that made Sabine laugh even more once she heard it. Who'd have thought that laughter could feel so good?

The doorbell rang and interrupted their good time. Mary grabbed a wad of cash off a table sitting next to the door and opened it, expecting the pizza delivery person to be on the other side. Her shoulders stiffened, and she spoke in a low tone, too quiet for Sabine to hear.

"Give her some damn time to get settled. You aren't welcome here right now." She slammed the door and turned to Sabine with a forced smile on her face. "Damn

Jehovah's Witnesses... It's like they know I'm a witch, so they're all over me and my guests always trying to hand me pamphlets about Jesus. One of these days, I'm going to move to the country where no one can find me."

Sabine's eyebrows crinkled as she studied Mary while she jabbered on about people bothering her. Raising the glass of wine to her lips, she inhaled the sweet smell before taking a sip. She was starting to feel it in her legs now as the calmness spread up her body from her toes.

The doorbell rang again, and this time, Mary stormed to the door and flung it open. She was ready to go to battle, but she found a smiling young lady balancing a pizza box with a couple of plastic containers on the other side.

Geez! She really has an aversion to solicitors. Sabine chuckled to herself as she finished her first glass of wine.

Mary brought in the food and set it down on the coffee table. "No use getting all formal. Let's just eat in here. I'll grab some paper plates."

"Sounds good. Do you want me to pour you another glass? I'm getting myself another."

"Hell, yeah," Mary said.

Two hours later, they were thoroughly stuffed with pizza and chocolate cake, feeling pretty good from the two bottles of wine they'd managed to drink their way through.

"I needed this. Thank you."

"My pleasure, honey. I told you that we had to stick together when we first met, didn't I?"

"Yes, you did."

"Just wish I hadn't done that damn spell for Remy now. Maybe none of this would've happened."

"Don't blame yourself. Bastian wanted me for his own. He just used that as an excuse to expedite the process. He would've gotten rid of Remy one way or another."

"You're right... Before I forget, you can sleep up in Sam's room. I'm sure she won't mind."

Sabine nodded. "I might go to bed shortly, if you don't care."

"Make yourself at home. It's your home now as long as you're here, so don't worry about asking if it's ok to do anything."

"What happened to the others staying here? Didn't you have people here when Remy and I came over?"

"They moved on when the vampire shenanigans in the form of Damen landed at the front door. It's just you and me for now."

"Thanks for everything." Sabine stood up, her legs shaking slightly as she tried to balance her weight. She bent down and kissed Mary on the head before going upstairs with her bags.

She shucked her clothing down to her panties. As she fished around in her bag for her grey nightgown, the sound of a slight exhalation of air caught her attention.

Grabbing her shirt and draping it in front of her, she whirled around to see a dark figure sitting in the corner of the room.

"Don't mind me. Nothing I haven't seen before." Remy's fingers laced together as his hands settled on the back of his head.

"What are you doing here?" Sabine pulled the shirt over her head, covering her naked torso.

"Just checking to see that you got here safely."

"It was you at the door earlier, wasn't it?"

"It was kind of rude of Mary to slam the door in my face like that. I was only going to offer to pay for your dinner."

"How noble of you."

"I try." The half-smile that made her go weak in the knees formed on his lips.

"Why are you really here? You just had my blood last night, so it isn't that."

"I missed you."

Putting her hand up, palm facing out, she said, "Don't."

"Don't what?"

"Don't do that. Don't act like you care."

"But I do care." His eyes softened into a pale green, not nearly as bright as they should be, but green nonetheless. "I don't know what's wrong with me." His eyes shifted and looked away from her as his hands dropped to his lap.

"Not falling for that one. Not after last night."

"*You* told me to pretend like I still cared…"

"Yes, and it's not a mistake I'll make again."

"What if it wasn't a lie, love?" Remy stood and closed the distance between them. Taking her hand, he peered down at her. "I don't know what's wrong with me, Beanie."

Her stomach fluttered when she heard the other name he used for her. He reserved this one for when he was trying to be sweet because he'd gotten it from her parents. She also hadn't heard it from him since before his 'death'.

Studying his face, she tried hard to find any hint of whether or not what he was saying was true. "I don't know what I can believe from you anymore." Shaking her head, she looked away.

"You must think I'm a nutter… Truth be told, I'm starting to question myself, too. The only thing I can say for sure is that I am still completely gobsmacked by you."

"English, please?"

"That *was* English, love. Oh, wait… I forgot you want me to Americanize my speech. Let's give that one a go again, shall we?"

She nodded. "Uh-huh."

His long fingers touched just underneath her chin and guided her to look at him again. "You must think I'm crazy, and I'm starting to believe it myself, but the one thing I know for sure is that I am still completely amazed by you."

"I do think you're crazy, Remy. You act as if you don't know me or what we had. You're downright mean to me at times."

"I am so sorry, love." He dropped to his knees and pressed the side of his face against her belly as he embraced her. "I keep having blackouts where I don't remember anything. Whole days have come and gone, and I have very little memory of them."

Running her fingers through his hair, she contemplated what to say or do. If he were being truthful, it meant that he wasn't completely lost to her, but he could be lying, and that meant he was the same prick he'd been since he came back from the dead.

"Remy..." Just as she spoke, his body stiffened and he fell to the ground into a fetal position. He gripped at his temples, trying hard to suppress a scream. "*Remy*? What's wrong?" Sabine dropped to his side and tried to shake him.

He rolled to his back and began laughing. His arms wrapped around his midsection as his eyes closed, and his body jerked from laughter. "Everything is fine..." he managed to say in the midst of the laughing fit. Remy sat up, his eyes peeping open.

She backed away from him as she saw the color of his eyes—black like coal and as cold as ice. "Mary!" she screamed.

"And just what do you think she is going to do, hmm?"

Moments later, Mary burst through the door. "You aren't welcome here anymore. Leave this house and don't come back."

His face contorted as anger seethed through his body. In an instant, he was gone.

"How did you do that?"

"He's not the only one with power around here. I have a spell on this house that will keep out those I don't want here. He just made the list."

"He did it again. I believed him."

"What happened?"

"Have you noticed he stopped using his weird words? The British slang, I mean. It's been completely gone."

"You're right. He's too formal when he speaks sometimes. And those eyes just freak me right the fuck out."

"When he spoke to me this time, he used some of his slang and he called me 'love' and 'Beanie'. He sounded like himself again, and his eyes weren't so... black."

"Have they changed back to green at all?"

"Twice before this... and his eyes have softened a couple of times. They were still dark, but not so black."

"When did they go back to green?"

"Once when we made lo—had sex."

"Girl, don't beat yourself up over sleeping with him. I can see it on your face. You regret it."

"I do, but only because I was fooled into believing I had him back when he was just pretending. The other time was right before we left. He kissed me and when he pulled back, his eyes were green. And then, just now, his eyes were pale green."

"So... during times when you two were getting physical and showing some kind of emotion, his eyes changed?"

"Yes."

"Hmmm..."

"I want so badly to believe that he's still in there, especially after the couple of dreams I've had, but I'm not sure there's anything left."

"Dreams?"

"Yeah... It's kind of our thing. We dream together," she said, not wanting to reveal all the details of their dreaming history. "I've had a couple of them recently where there are two of him. One of them tells me not to trust the other one, and Remy was in chains in the last one. It's probably just my subconscious trying to make sense of things, but I can't shake the feeling that it's really him."

"Maybe it is him, though." A twinkle passed over Mary's eyes as she headed toward the door. "Come with me downstairs." They made their way to the basement and over to a huge bookcase. Retrieving a thick, leather-bound book, Mary sat down in a chair and motioned for Sabine to sit beside her. "What if he's been possessed by Nicas instead of just revived by his power?"

"Holy hell, why didn't I think of that before? That's probably the real reason he kept talking like he was. He wasn't talking about himself when kept saying 'he' and 'him'."

"I don't want to get your hopes up in case I'm wrong, but it makes sense, doesn't it?"

"How can we find out?"

"I can try to conjure Nicas if I can find the spell I need. It should be in this book. If he's on the other side where he should be, I'll be able to reach him."

"Then what?"

"Well, if he isn't there, we exorcise the hell out of Remy and hope we can kick Nicas' ass to the curb, but I need your help. You have to tap into the magic that lies inside of you because exorcising someone isn't a task just one witch should do. It's too dangerous."

"That could take years though. Doesn't it take centuries for a witch to master her magic?"

"That's only partly true. It takes years to get to the point where a witch can create spells and use magic without really thinking about it, but anyone can take advantage of spells that are already made and tap into their natural magical abilities. It just takes more time and effort. They just have to believe. That's how you were able to do the cloaking spell."

"But what if I can't do any of that? I mean, how can anyone just become a witch?"

"Every human being has magic inside them. Magic is responsible for things that we sometimes take for granted."

"Like what?"

"Emotions... Imagination... Imagination *is* magic. Learn to tap the power behind your emotions or imagination, and you've got it made, babe."

"Okay, new plan. We start this tonight. I don't want to put it off another day."

"Alright, I want you to practice blocking everything out. That really is the best place for you to start. I can teach you all kinds of spells, but in order to use the magic within and master the more complicated spells, you have to be able to start there so you have no interference. The kind of magic you're going to need to help me with requires it. Once you've got that down, we'll start with some simple spells and work our way up over the next few weeks."

"Can you teach me a locator spell? Would that be an easy one?"

"Sure. Who or what do you want to find?"

"My family. They've disappeared."

Mary shook her head and snickered. "I do not envy you, girl. So much bullshit going on in your life. Time to change things for the better. The locator spell will be step two then."

CHAPTER 11

A few days later, Mary had finally found the spell and almost everything she needed to conjure Nicas. She unlocked a large cabinet and began rummaging through its contents while Sabine waited patiently. She was torn between whether or not she wanted Nicas to come forward. On the one hand, if he didn't, then that most likely meant their suspicions were true and Remy was possessed. However, if he did come forward, then maybe they could go the much easier route of simply binding some of his powers. They'd be able to see if restraining him would bring the true Remy forth.

"I know that damn thing is in here somewhere. I really need to go through all this crap and organize it all." Mary continued to rifle through papers, trinkets, and other random things. Her hand felt around the top shelf, too high for her to see if what she was looking for was there. "Ah-ha! There it is." She quickly yanked down a deep crimson stone with white markings etched in it.

"What is that?"

"This is the talisman of the dead. Not many of them still exist, but this old witch is one of the lucky few to have one. I got it from my mother, of all people. I ought to summon her ass and see what she has to say for herself."

"Do it! You never know what she might do."

"That's just it. I don't know what she'd do. Even though she's dead, she's still very powerful. And she'd do anything for Bastian," her eyes shifted away from

Sabine, "even if that meant giving up on her own daughter."

"I'm sorry, Mary."

"I'll just say I won't rule it out."

"Fair enough. Do you need my help? Not that I can do all that much anyway…"

"You can observe so you have a reference if you should ever need to conjure someone." Mary grabbed a canister of salt and tossed it to Sabine. "Here is something you can do. Measure out two cups of that and mix it with two cups of sand. I have a big box of it over there under that desk. Go grab a mixing bowl from the kitchen."

Sabine did as she was told and returned to Mary with the mixture.

"Take this book and sit down in the middle of the floor there." Mary began making a thick line on the floor out of the salt and sand mixture. "This is for protection. Even though you won't be helping me with the spell, I still want you safe. You never know what sort of devil might hitch a ride when conjuring the dead."

"Yeah, I have no desire to meet anyone or anything like that. I've got enough shit going on in my life at the moment."

Mary completed the circle, placed five candles in different places within the confined space, and sat down next to Sabine. With the flick of her wrist, they all lit. She grabbed the spell book from Sabine and opened it to the page she required. "All the words are in this book. All I have to do is tap into my power and say them as I hold the talisman of the dead over the flame. If Nicas is on the other side, he'll show up pretty fast. If he isn't, well, then we'll have to figure out how to trap Remy so we can exorcise him."

Mary's eyes darkened as she stared off at nothing for just a split second. She began chanting words that were foreign to Sabine. The only words she could make out was 'Nicas Lordanescu'.

A breeze began to blow through the windowless basement. Goose bumps spread over Sabine's flesh as the hair on her arms pricked up. An eerie, vibrating hum radiated throughout the basement. As the hum became louder, she realized it was voices of the disembodied kind. She hoped like hell the layer of salt making up the circle really would protect them from evil.

Mary's eyes cleared, and the hum stopped. "He isn't there." She smiled widely at Sabine.

* * *

A quiet buzzing of her cell phone caught her attention as she tried hard to block everything out. Sabine had tried and tried to master this one simple step, but her thoughts were too busy. The lyrics to her favorite Ferrum song would play through her head or she'd hear a car horn outside and that was it. She'd lose it and then feel like she was failing Mary and Remy.

She reached over to the nightstand and picked up the phone. Sam hadn't called for a few days, so she wasn't surprised to hear from her.

"Hey chica, what's up?"

"Nothing much. Just wanted to check in. My mom and I have been hanging out doing a lot of mother-daughter things."

"That's great! I'm so happy you two were able to reunite."

"Well, we have you to thank for that. If it weren't for you, I'd still think she was dead… which is the real reason I wanted to talk to you."

Dread coursed through her body as she waited for Sam to continue.

"Ok, so here it goes. I was thinking about your family and how they've just up and disappeared. I was telling my mom a little about it since my grandparents left with me right after she came here. I told her how you went to your house and they were just gone. She had some interesting things to say."

"Like?"

"Well, like we disappeared kind of the same way, and she says another offering before her had family that up and left, too. She says Brendon was always a little bonkers and never mentioned anything about his family."

"He's done something to them." The urge to find her family went into overdrive. Where the hell were they? And what exactly had Bastian done to them? Gut clenching as it threatened to spill the contents of her lunch, she doubled over for a second before regaining her composure.

"I mentioned to you how my grandparents had always said my mother died. What if they weren't saying it to protect me from the truth, and he just made them think she died? Fuck, can you imagine going through the loss of a child that wasn't really lost?"

She was so shocked by the revelation that she almost forgot to breathe. Sabine inhaled sharply. "They think I'm dead," she said with a tremble in her voice.

She knew it in her heart. There was no need for confirmation or further investigation. She had to find them as soon as possible and prove to them that she was alive and well. The thought of going through life without them as they mourned her was the final straw in the shitstorm of her life. She *had* to get this magic thing down even if it drove her insane in the process.

"I need to go, Sam. I have to focus."

"I know, but before I let you go, there's one more thing I want to tell you, and it's actually good news."

"Lay it on me. I need to hear something good for once."

"Remy has agreed to release Mom. He's even buying us a house in Willow Creek to live in."

Her heart smiled, and she felt a sense of accomplishment that he'd taken her suggestion seriously. Even if he wasn't himself all the time, at least she knew he really was still in there somewhere.

"That's wonderful, Sam!"

"I'll let you go now before we end up talking for an hour," Sam said with a chuckle. "You've got important work to do."

"Oh, Sam, you have no idea. I'll fill you in on everything when I see you again."

As the girls ended their conversation, Sabine assessed her situation.

Remy is possessed by an ancient vampire... the ancient vampire, I should say. I have to become an all-powerful witch because said ancient vampire wants to use me as he pleases. The real reason I need to become an all-powerful witch is because I need to save the man I love from the ancient asshat. My parents think I'm dead. Again, being a witch would be uber helpful in finding them. Bastian is still on the loose with that evil fucktard Brendon. Even if he isn't a vampire, he's still a psycho that I have no desire to ever encounter again... What else could go wrong?

* * *

"Damn it, girl. You're not trying hard enough," Mary said, throwing her hands up in the air with exasperation.

"I'm trying!" Sabine sat in the middle of the basement floor with a lit candle in front of her. "I'm sorry but I think it'd be a hell of a lot easier to blow out the damn flame than to magically poof it away."

"Well, no shit, Sherlock. But where would that get you as far as learning magic?"

"Nowhere, I suppose."

"Then just do it already."

"I know why it isn't working."

"Oh, yeah? Enlighten me…"

"I could just blow it out."

Mary sighed. "We just had this conversation five seconds ago."

Sabine chuckled. "What I'm trying to say is this isn't working for me because the easier solution doesn't involve magic. Give me something that would be easier to use magic to accomplish than to just do it myself… Like have me pick up a car or something."

A loud cackle burst out of Mary. "You little dummy!"

"Hey! I am not a dummy!" Sabine stood, dramatically placing her hands on her hips while she tried hard not to laugh. "Ok, so maybe not lifting a car, but you get what I'm saying, right?"

"I do. That actually isn't a bad idea, but if you fuck up and the damn car goes rolling away, then what the hell do we do? I don't think insurance covers magical disasters."

"Probably not."

Four months had passed since Sabine moved to Mary's. One thing she knew for sure was that eagerness wasn't all you needed to use magic. Eagerness, she had plenty of. There was nothing more she wanted than to be able to fix Remy and to find her family. What she didn't have plenty of was any magical abilities to show for it.

Her attempt at location spells for her family had even gone belly up, though that wasn't totally her fault. Mary hadn't had much luck either, mainly because Sabine only had a picture and not anything that actually belonged to her family. The closest they had come was figuring out that her family was somewhere in Pennsylvania. The state as a whole was circled with the herbs they used for the spell instead of a pinpointed location. She needed something more personal to narrow down the search, but where she was going to get anything like that now, she didn't know.

She'd left most of her stuff behind, thinking she could bring more once she got settled in at the Manor. Remy had convinced her this would be best. Little did she know, he'd actually had a plan to set her free and thought she'd be back with her family in no time. That wasn't what happened at all, but looking back, she wondered if maybe it would've been for the best. Sure, she would've missed him, but maybe she'd been able to move on with her life by now. Maybe she wouldn't be doing everything she could to get him back, even though she wasn't sure at times that he could truly be saved.

"Let me think on it, and I'll find something else for you to try, but in the meantime, keep trying with the flame."

"Alright. I'm taking it up to my room."

"Uh-huh. You better not be asleep if I come in there fifteen minutes from now."

"I promise." Sabine blew out the flame, grabbed the candle and matches, and headed up to her room to practice. She half-expected Remy to be waiting on her when she got back, but he wasn't. He was due for a feeding and would be popping up any time now.

He pretty much avoided the front door since Mary didn't want him there in the first place and had reluctantly allowed him back in. She only had because, even though she hated to admit it, Remy scared her with his seemingly endless supply of power and abilities, and she didn't want to test him too much. After all, they were fairly confident that it was Nicas they were dealing with after failing to reach him.

Since he no longer used the front door, he was forced to use other means of entry. The light tapping on the window or him materializing in her room reminded her so much of times past when he would show up at her parent's house back when he was tasked with keeping her alive and unharmed until she turned twenty-one.

The weather had become cooler as summer gave way to autumn. Sabine loved opening her window and letting the crisp air of the afternoon flow through her room. As she slid the window up, the sound of a familiar voice broke the silence. She instinctively turned, thinking he had come in without her noticing, but the room was still empty.

Realizing that Remy was outside talking to someone on a cell phone, she casually sat down next to the window to eavesdrop on his conversation. She used her newfound technique of quieting her mind in order to really hear him. It was an amazing trick to use when she wanted to focus on a particular thing because she could block out whatever noise she deemed unnecessary. It might have taken her two months to master it, but she was proud of her accomplishment.

"Yes, I've decided to purchase the one on Walnut Street we talked about... That's right. It'll be in her name alone. It's a gift... No, not that one, the one with the patio on the back and the big yard with the willow tree... I'm not in Willow Creek right now, but I can come by tomorrow to complete the paperwork... I'm certain they'll accept my offer. Will they be there as well?"

My house is on Walnut. I can't believe he wants to buy my *house with* my *willow tree for Sam.* Her hands fisted at her side. Rage started to grow deep in her belly. Not because she didn't want the best for Sam and her mother, but because it was another slap in the face by him. *Why am I fighting so hard for him again?*

"That's unfortunate... Okay. I'll see you tomorrow." He slid his finger across the screen, ended the call, and glanced toward her window. His eyes met hers and before she had time to look away, he stood before her.

"You look angry. What is it now?"

"Really? You're buying my house?"

"I'm not."

"I just heard you! You were talking to someone about buying the house on Walnut with the willow tree."

"Well, what do we have here? Someone has developed a keen sense of hearing, haven't they? Those magic lessons are really starting to pay off, hmm?"

She turned away from him in disgust, focusing on the candle as she spoke. "Sam has told me numerous times about house hunting with you. I know it's for her."

"It is for her, but it isn't your house. You know the town is called 'Willow Creek' for a reason... Yours isn't the only house on that street that has one."

Her knuckles went white as she gripped the edges of the dresser, still focusing on the candle. Choosing to focus on the candle had more to do with not wanting to look at him than it did with anything else. She hadn't even bothered to light the wick, so it was pointless trying to put it out with her mind.

"Any luck finding your parents?"

"No. Any luck finding Bastian?"

"I haven't been looking."

Anger slammed into her, amping up the feelings of rage already present. "Yeah, why bother, right? He's only the best way of finding out exactly where my family is. No biggie." Her eyes narrowed as her brows drew together, still looking at the wick of the candle. Her cheeks flushed as the rage began to radiate through her body.

He moved closer to her, hand sliding up her back to rest at the nape of her neck. "I'm hungry," he breathed into her ear, "and I want you."

They'd slept together a half a dozen times since she came to Mary's. She hated herself afterward every time. It was Nicas she was ultimately having sex with, and she knew that, even though he always lied to her during the

109

act with his beautiful, green eyes. Desperate for a connection with her love, she gave in too many times. *Not this time.*

A spark flickered, igniting the wick of the candle. She gasped and stepped back. "Did you see that?" A feeling of glee overtook her at the realization that *she* had caused the candle to light.

"I'm impressed. I wasn't sure you really had it in you."

"I wasn't even trying to light it. I was just trying to focus on anything but you."

"Glad I could help, now come here." He took her hand softly in his, leading her over to the bed.

"I'm not fucking you, Remy. Not anymore."

His eyes flashed green as he smiled sweetly at her. "I don't want to fuck you, either. I want to make love to you."

"Just stop. That's not going to work anymore. I only end up hurting the next day for giving in to you. Bite me and go."

"You know what? I'm suddenly not in the mood for your blood. I'll find someone else to indulge on."

"Fine by me."

He hesitated, calling her bluff. When she didn't waver, he disappeared through the window.

The thought of him feeding, or more, on someone other than her didn't settle well with her, but she couldn't keep giving into him. Not until he was himself again.

"Mary, you have to come here," Sabine shouted. She focused on the flame she had created and began to play with it. The more she focused, the bigger it grew.

The door swung open. Mary watched her with bright eyes and a jaw that began to drop. "I knew you could do it! How did you learn to control it?"

"Through anger, rage, and guilt."

"Yep, those will usually do it. I'm so proud of you... Now we just gotta get you to that point without feeling like shit first."

* * *

Remy got into his car, slamming the door shut and speeding off down the road. Trying to find someone else to feed from wasn't something he wanted to do, though he knew he could pick up some fresh-faced college girl on the Pitt campus easy enough. It was a quick drive from Mary's to Oakland, and there would be plenty to choose from. All it would take would be a flash of a smile and words laced with his Londoner accent. Women went nuts over it, especially American women.

I'll starve if I can't have her.

He'd only threatened picking up someone else, hoping she would give in. Those times with her were the only times he felt as if he were completely in control of himself, like he'd been able to break free from whatever it was that was holding him back. She pulled him out of

111

the darkness and cleared his mind when they connected, not only physically, but also on an emotional level, and he was able to keep the dark entity away for much longer after their encounters.

He longed for the taste of her blood as it had been the first time he had her. It was sweet and flowed like warm honey down his throat the night they married. It was then that he convinced himself that he *could* live on only her, despite what he'd initially thought when the pairing was announced. Though her blood was still almost sickeningly sweet, the last few months, the taste had altered. A bitterness had crept in and began tainting the love that flowed through her. The only explanation could be that she was falling out of love with him, and who could blame her?

What in the bloody hell am I going to do if she ends up hating me? I have to keep moving forward with my plan and hope that I can shake the thing in the dark.

CHAPTER 12

"You're going to have to seduce him," Mary said matter-of-factly.

"There has to be some other way."

"I'm not deaf, honey. I know there's been a little somethin', somethin' going on up there at times between you two."

"Yes, but not for a while now. He hasn't even been back to feed since last week. I pissed him off when I told him I wouldn't do anything with him."

"That's perfect! You can play it like you want to make it up to him."

"Okay, but then what? Do I actually have to go through with it?"

"No, but the closer you are to it, the less focused he'll be, and I can subdue him easier."

Mary and Sabine had decided that it was time to exorcise Remy even though Sabine wasn't nearly as powerful as Mary had hoped she'd be. Fortunately, she'd come across a spell to temporarily boost a witch's powers, and she was confident she could do the exorcism herself with the boost. All Sabine needed to do was help get Remy into position and chant a few specific lines throughout the process.

"How am I supposed to get him in the basement? He'll be expecting me in my room."

The basement was a hot spot of sorts for magical occurrences. Though Mary could perform spells and use her magic in other places, she preferred to be as close to the earth as she could. Dirt was an excellent conductor of magic. What better place for such an in-depth spell than below ground in a basement?

"I'll go outside to boost myself. I can go just behind the tree line back there so no one will see me. I'll wait until he comes into the house before I start. Text him and say you're practicing in the basement. Trust me, if he thinks he's gonna get with you, he'll go wherever you are. Just make sure you stay in that circle. Hopefully, we've made it big enough that he won't notice it around the edges of the room."

"I'll text him now." She grabbed her phone from her pocket and began typing a message to Remy.

I'm sorry about last week. I miss you.

Seconds ticked by as she waited for a response. Finally, it came through.

I've missed you as well. Shall I come over?

Yes. Please hurry...

I'll be there in a few minutes. I won't bother driving.

Mary isn't here. I'm in the basement practicing, so just come in.

Mary hurried out of the house and to a thin line of trees that separated her property from a local city park, waiting for him to appear.

He descended from the sky and stood by the front door, assessing the area. She watched him cautiously, ready to react to protect herself if necessary.

Come on, you son of a bitch. Don't get suspicious now.

He walked up to the door and turned the knob, disappearing inside.

* * *

Her heart beat against the inside of her chest in anticipation. Footsteps coming down the stairs alerted her to his presence. She stood, waiting for him to come to her. Trying hard to mask her trembling hands, she wrapped them around her body as she crossed her arms in front of her.

He hesitated just at the foot of the stairs and looked down. *Oh, shit. He sees the salt.*

"Planning on making some magic with me tonight?" He smirked and stepped over the line of salt on the floor. "We don't need any protective barrier though. I'm all the protection you need."

"It's just there because I've been practicing."

"No matter... Take off your clothes."

"Um, excuse me?"

"You called me here for a specific purpose, did you not?"

"I'm not opposed to it. I just thought we'd reconnect a little first." She was trying hard to stall so Mary would have plenty of time to complete her spell, and she had very little desire to actually go through the actual act with him.

"We can reconnect with no clothes on." He flashed a grin at her as he slid his black shirt up over his head, exposing his torso. "Your turn."

Her fingers shook as she unbuttoned the top two buttons of her shirt, exposing the purple pendant that had belonged to his mother. His eyes locked onto it and he stepped back, almost stumbling over his own feet.

"What's wrong?" She reached out to touch him, but he only stepped back once again.

"That's my... Bloody hell..." he said, falling to his knees.

Sabine rushed to his side. "Are you alright?"

His eyes, glistening red, focused on the pendant. She watched as the blackness in them faded away.

"Remy, look at me," she said loudly, grabbing his chin and tilting it toward her. "Are you alright?"

"I am now, love." A bloody tear slid down his cheek as he kissed her hand. "You have no idea how hard I've been fighting to get back to you. Every time I've tried to really talk to you, I've been ripped away."

She wanted to believe him, but he'd lied so many times now that she couldn't allow herself to fall for it again. "You don't have to do this. You don't have to lie anymore."

He looked at her with a dumbfounded expression on his face. "I'm not lying. I've never lied when we were together."

"You're lying right now! You pretend to be the man I fell in love with every time we have sex, and I'm not falling for it. I know I told you to, and it was a mistake."

"It was always me. Don't you see?"

"I see your face, your eyes... I also see the monster peeking out from behind them." The faint sound of the door closing caught her attention. *This is it. Mary is going to fix you.* "It ends now, Nicas."

"Nicas?"

Footsteps on the stairs caught her attention. She whirled around to see Damen walking down them instead of Mary. "Mary is gone. Someone has taken her."

"Who took her?" Sabine asked, hurrying over to Damen. "And why in the hell are you here?"

"I was in the area and thought I'd stop by to see how you were doing. Sam asked me to, so I thought I'd be nice... I saw her out behind the trees, and the next thing I knew, someone had taken her. I really don't want to say who took her. There has to be some mistake or some misunderstanding."

"Who was it?" Sabine asked through clenched teeth.

"Gretchen."

Sabine gasped, turning around to see Remy, confusion etched on his face. "Why would she do this?"

Remy stayed motionless, as if he hadn't heard her question.

"What's up with him?" Damen asked, gesturing in Remy's direction.

"He's being a dick."

"Shocker," Damen muttered.

"Why won't you believe me?" Remy looked at her, lines of confusion gathered on his forehead.

"I don't believe you because you've pulled this shit before. More times than I can count."

"Okay, someone want to fill me in?" Damen asked, sitting down in a nearby chair.

Sabine swallowed hard, knowing she had to tell the truth in order to get everything all out on the table. She'd already confessed to knowing Nicas was in control of Remy. There was no going back now.

"He's been possessed by Nicas, and he's pretending not to know at the moment. Mary and I were going to exorcise him. She was outside preparing." She cautiously looked at Remy. He sat with his knees bent up toward his chest. His head hung between them.

"I've told you, I'm not bloody lying, Sabine. Why can't you see that?"

Damen leaned forward. "How do you know he isn't telling the truth?"

"I just do."

"I'd never give up on you, love. I don't know why you've given up on me so easily."

"Really? I've done nothing but fight for you since Bastian locked you up in the first place. You're the one who has completely changed... I can't even deal with this bullshit right now." She turned to Damen. "Please go find Mary."

"Would if I could... Gretchen grabbed her, and they vanished. There's no way to follow. She's gone. And thanks to him forcing Mary to sever the tie between him and Gretchen, he can't find her either. How's that whole unbinding everyone thing workin' for ya?" Damen sneered.

Remy stood suddenly, closing the gap between him and Sabine. He looked at her with fire and determination in his eyes as he cupped her cheek with one hand. "I'll prove to you it's really me. I'm going to do everything in my power to find her."

"Just leave. I don't want to look at you." Sabine tilted her head away. In her gut, she felt like he was making the situation about himself, and it was about him before, but now it was about finding Mary and getting her back.

"I'm not leaving you here alone. It isn't safe," Remy said.

"I don't feel all that safe with you either if I'm being honest."

"Fine, you don't have to stay with me, but at least let me take you somewhere that's safer than this." He grabbed her around the waist, pulling her close. The space around them began to contort and buzz with static electricity. She closed her eyes and clung to him, knowing what to expect next. Teleporting made her dizzy and nauseated, but at least if she had time to close her eyes, it cut down on those nasty little side effects.

Damen stood and looked around as they disappeared in front of his eyes. "Don't worry about me, guys... I'll just be over here, wondering what the fuck is going on."

CHAPTER 13

The discombobulating feeling of teleporting faded away quickly, thanks in part to her being able to prepare herself. She was keenly aware that her body melded to his perfectly as they stood there together in silence, despite the difference in height. As he held her tight, she lingered in his arms before opening her eyes. For a few seconds, she could pretend they were back to how things had been before when he was hers, she was his, and no one had succeeded in tearing them apart. Once her eyes were open, the illusion that everything was fine and as it should be would melt away. She wasn't ready for that to happen.

His hand grazed the back of her head, tangling strands of her hair in his fingers. "Beanie, look where you are."

"Don't call me that," she whispered. Her eyes cracked open to find a dimly lit room illuminated by a street lamp outside. She stepped back, allowing her eyes a second to adjust. Her stomach knotted as the sensation of butterflies erupted. "Why bring me here?"

"Because no one would think to look for you here now."

The comforting smell of her bedroom, her home, overwhelmed her. It was all too much, and she reached out for the bed to steady herself. "Someone else must live here now," she said while looking around at all the furnishings that hadn't been there the last time she was. "It doesn't belong to my parents anymore."

"No… it belongs to you, love. I had it furnished so that it would be ready to live in once I gave you the keys. No one but the realtor knows I've purchased this, so you should be safe here. Just stay quiet and don't go outside for the time being. I understand why you don't want to be around me, but I still want to keep you safe. I'll bring you some food, but then I'll leave you alone."

Her heart dropped to her stomach, her head scrambled with confusion. What were his intentions? Had he decided to let her go? "I don't understand why you did this."

"It wasn't always him you were dealing with." And with that, he was gone.

Could it really be him? Why else would he do this? Only my Remy would do something like this for me. But what's happened to Nicas if it really is Remy now?

Closing the blinds, she lit the bedside lamp and looked around. She'd failed to notice that three of her paintings, which she thought she'd left behind when she went to Willow Creek Manor to live, hung on the wall next to posters of her favorite rock star, Ash London. *He must have sent for them before they left.* The closet door stood open, and to her surprise, it was filled with new shoes, clothes, and handbags. Most of the items were simple like she wore most days, but she was sure some of the others had come from the closet at the Manor by the looks of how elegant they were.

She rummaged through the drawers of a vanity table that sat against the far wall to find new cosmetics, perfumes, and girly stuff in general. Most of the products

122

were higher-end brands that she'd never used before, like Dolce & Gabbana, Dior, Urban Decay, and Smashbox. A drawer full of Cover Girl would have thrilled her, but this was pretty sweet. The whole thing was sweet. Too sweet for Nicas to pull off by himself. She couldn't believe the thought he'd put into the things he'd provided for her. Would Nicas have thought to do all of this or was it really Remy? Confused didn't begin to describe how she felt.

As much as she wanted to explore the rest of the house and its furnishings, she thought it best to stay put in her bedroom. Too much moving around and turning on lights might draw unwanted attention. She needed to eat because it had been hours since she'd had anything. He'd mentioned bringing her food, which indicated there was none in the house. There was no way she could actually eat anything anyway with her stomach threatening to back up on her at any second. *Puking in* my *house just doesn't seem like the thing to do at the moment... Jesus, I'm home.*

* * *

The feeling he had while perching himself on the branch in the willow tree outside her room had nostalgia written all over it. He couldn't be inside with her, but as long as he was in control, he was going to make damn sure she was safe. This meant going back to a time when he silently watched her, making sure she didn't find herself in danger from outside threats. He'd protected her from harm then, and he'd do it again. Though he felt like himself again, the power and abilities he'd possessed from Nicas were still coursing through him. *If someone wants her, they'll have to go through me, and there's no bloody way that'll happen. I won't allow it.*

He couldn't take the chance that she wasn't a target after Mary had been abducted. *Why the bloody hell would Gretchen take her? What does she want with her? Perhaps she's trying to have a go at me for cutting her loose so easily, but she'd have to have known I was sending Sabine to train under Mary, and very few people knew of my plan. Unless she's been spying all this time.*

He vaguely remembered being cruel to Gretchen not long after he'd turned her, and he regretted it immensely. What he did wasn't right, and he hoped he could make it up to her. But if she was somehow plotting something against him, the opportunity might have passed by all too soon.

As he sat outside Sabine's window, listening to her moving around her room in awe of the things he'd left for her, he tried to recall other memories. Most everything from the moment he snapped Nicas' neck was a blur, save for the times he connected with Sabine. He could see flashes of things that'd happened, but not much came through clear enough to vividly remember.

His thoughts turned toward what he could do to make her happy while she was in hiding. He didn't have any leads on her family. Purchasing the house from them had been his best one, yet it turned up cold when the realtor had explained that his company had purchased the home from the Crowley's and didn't have recent contact information for them. *What else can I do?*

The one thing he could do slammed into him like a brick. Summoning Damen, he waited patiently for him to arrive. Once he did, Remy jumped down to the ground and issued his instructions.

"Stay here and keep an eye on her. Make sure no one gets to her. If you sit up there in the branch closest to her window, you'll be able to hear if anything becomes suspicious."

Damen nodded, sprung into the tree with little effort, and settled himself in.

Remy raced through the neighborhood until he came to the little, white house. Walking up to the front door, he rang the bell.

"I'll get it!" He heard a female say from the other side of the door just before it swung open.

"Remy," Lana, one of Sabine's best friends, exclaimed. Lana and her other best friend, Delia, hadn't really disappeared, though they'd eventually cut off communication with Sabine as abruptly as her family had. Delia moved to New York City in pursuit of a Broadway career while Lana stayed behind to continue going to college in Morgantown. She was only home this particular night because she'd come to visit her parents for the weekend, like she often did.

She stepped outside and onto the porch. Pursing her lips together, she tilted her head. "I'm so sorry."

"For?"

"For your loss. It's been hard for all of us. I just can't believe she's gone." Lana's eyes began to water as a fountain of tears threatened to let loose. "I never thought she'd kill herself."

He stepped closer to Lana, placing a hand on her shoulder. "Lana, dear... Sabine isn't dead, and she certainly didn't off herself. Who told you that?"

"*What*?" Lana suddenly leaned against the house to steady herself. "But we saw her. We all went to her funeral. Delia even came back for it."

"That's not possible. She is alive and well right now. I'll take you to her."

"Okay, are you in denial or something? I'm telling you, I *saw* her in her casket. It was white with silver accents. She's buried in the cemetery up the road. I know because I visit her every time I come back to Willow Creek." Tears dripped down her cheeks as her lip began to quiver. "I bring her lilies. They're her favorite..."

Remy wrapped his arms around her, allowing her to cry into his shoulder. "Shhh... Please, don't cry. I'm not making this up, and I'm not in denial. Now tell me, who told you she killed herself?"

She looked up at him, whispering, "Bastian."

He caught her in a trance. "I need you to tell me exactly what he told you."

Her face went blank. No more emotion, just a stone-cold stare as she spoke. "He told me she hung herself in the closet and that you had found her. You were so devastated that you left town. He said I would remember going to her funeral and that she was in a white casket with silver accents. The whole town showed up for her

126

funeral. He paid for a headstone for her in the cemetery and told me where to find it. He also took my phone and gave me a brand new one with a new number when he told me she died, but he didn't say why, only that I didn't need my old one anymore."

"Yeah, he lied to you, and you know that now."

Her pupils dilated and quickly returned to their normal size. "Oh my God... Can I see her?"

"Absolutely, but could I trouble you for some food? I'm sure she's hungry, and she has none at the moment."

"Hang on!" Lana disappeared inside the house and came back a few minutes later carrying a plastic bag full of snacks and a sandwich she'd thrown together.

"Do you trust me not to hurt you?"

Without hesitation, Lana said, "Yes."

"Hang on." He scooped her up and took off like a flash back to Sabine's. Once they arrived, he sat her down on her feet and helped her steady herself.

"You'll likely be dizzy for a few minutes. Before we go in, can I ask you something?"

Lana shook her head like she was shaking loose the dizziness. "Sure, but make it quick. I can't wait to see her."

"Do you know where her family is?"

Lana's face sunk as the realization hit her that Sabine's family was unnecessarily mourning her death.

"They left town right after it happened."

"Do you know where they went?"

"Not exactly, but I could find out. I still talk to her sister sometimes."

"Find out, but don't say anything to her. I don't want to get her hopes up if we can't find them."

"Will you make them see the truth like you did me?"

He nodded, pulling out a key to the front door. Just as he unlocked it, he turned back to her. "Stay behind me. I want to surprise her."

Damen dropped down from his perch. Lana jumped back, stifling a screech.

"Sorry. Didn't mean to scare you... I'm going back to Mary's. If she wanted Sabine, too, she'll go back."

"All right. Let me know anything you see or hear that might lead us to Mary."

Remy walked through the door and up the stairs. Lana stayed back just enough to be hidden in the dark. He tapped on Sabine's door. "It's me..."

The door slowly opened as she peeked out through a crack before opening it all the way. "Come in."

"There's something I want to show you." He turned and motioned for Lana to step forward so Sabine could see her. "I have someone who has brought you some food to eat."

As Lana came into Sabine's view, she was taken aback by her friend. Why was she here now and not ignoring her altogether?

"Sabine! I thought you were…" Lana threw her arms around Sabine and squeezed her as hard as she could. Trying to speak through the sobbing, she found it difficult to say what she wanted to say.

"I think what our dear Lana is trying to say is that she thought you were dead."

"Then it's true… That sick sonofabitch… Oh, Lana, I'm so sorry!" Sabine squeezed her back, and the two girls fell to the floor laughing through tears over their unexpected reunion.

Remy smiled to himself and quietly sat down in a chair across the room, giving them space to reunite. He knew he couldn't leave because there were too many questions that needed answers, and Sabine would start asking them as soon as she was able to compose herself.

Once Sabine and Lana had a chance to reconnect, Sabine glanced at Remy and said, "Sam and I figured it out before that Bastian must have told my parents I was dead. I just had no idea he told my friends that, too."

"He would've had to. Otherwise, we'd have thought they were crazy if they talked about you like you were dead when we knew better," Lana said. "Who is Sam?"

"Sam is a good friend I made after I moved. When I quit hearing from you and Delia, it was nice to have someone to talk to. Our paths crossed, and we really hit it off."

Lana frowned and fidgeted with her hair. "I'm so sorry. I feel awful that you felt so alone. At least you had Remy, right?" She smiled brightly as she glanced back and forth between the two, who could barely look at each other.

"Yes, and no… It's a long story."

"I've got time. I'm not leaving right away."

"Well, Remy was locked up by Bastian, Bastian tried to take me as his own, but Remy was able to stop him. I thought he was dead, turns out he wasn't, but he's not been himself since then, and we aren't really together anymore… in a nutshell. Did I forget anything?"

"You forgot that I still love you," Remy said, spreading a thick layer of awkwardness on the situation.

Lana giggled like she was sometimes prone to do in weird situations. "At least you had Sam. I can't wait to meet her." Lana smiled warmly at Sabine as she tried to change the subject.

"She lives just down the street a ways," Remy said. "I'm sure she'd run right over if you called her. Then you lot can have a slumber party with pajamas, make overs, and all that girly shit," he said sarcastically. "Stuff yourselves with pizza and ice cream and then talk about the boys you'll never have while completely ignoring the man right in front of you." He knew he was out of line, but he couldn't stand that Sabine seemed to hate him now. He couldn't really blame her, but the fact that she'd lost faith and seemed to give up on him cut deep. Her summary of the events leading up to where they currently were left out some rather important moments, and it hurt to know she'd gloss over them like they were insignificant. "I'll leave you to it."

As she watched him start to leave, Sabine said, "Remy, wait…" but before she could get a response, he was gone.

"What was all that about?" Lana asked. "You guys were so in love and happy before."

"It's complicated."

"Want to talk about it?"

"No… I want to know what you've been up to. I need to hear what normal people are doing nowadays and forget about all the bullshit I've been going through."

"Okay, but are you sure you don't want to go after him?"

Sabine sat in silence for a moment as she pondered her response. "No, it isn't safe for me to leave." She knew she didn't have to go far if she wanted to talk to him. He was right outside, perched in the tree most likely. If he truly did care about her, that was where he'd be.

CHAPTER 14

Early the next morning, Remy tapped on the window a few times before getting Sabine's attention. She ambled over to the window, sliding it up. Finding him looking just as tired as she felt, she stepped aside so he could come in.

"I'm exhausted and need to sleep."

"Why are you so tired? You don't normally get worn out so easily."

"I haven't fed, if you must know, but I do generally need to sleep sometimes."

As untrusting of him as she was, she felt bad that he hadn't eaten. "If you're hungry, then feed from me. It's what my destiny in life is after all."

"No. I'll just sleep it off."

"Remy... will we ever be able to fix us?"

"That depends on you, love. I'm ready and willing, yet you still don't see that I'm me."

"I've been through such a roller coaster with you these last few months. I've wanted so much to bring you out of it, and you've fooled me numerous times. I just don't know what to believe."

"You don't get it," he exclaimed. "I *need* you, Sabine... Every second since the sight of you wearing my mother's necklace brought me back, I can feel darkness coming for me. It's picking at my mind, clawing its way in. I'm fighting so hard to stay here with you, but if I'm being honest, it seems like a much easier time just to let it take me. If I thought you'd be any better off, I would."

She moved closer to him, placing one arm around his back, guiding him to the bed. "Lay down."

Lying on the bed, he began to stare at the ceiling. Her body shifted the mattress as she sat next to him. Her hand slid behind his head, propping it up while she wedged her shoulder into the space between him and the pillow so that his face rested against her chest. He turned into her, his hand lying gently on her belly, and closed his eyes. Listening to the steady sound of her breath and the thumping of her heart lulled him into a deep sleep.

When he awakened later that night, the sounds that had put him to sleep were still going strong. She'd stayed with him all day and now slept peacefully beside him. He sat up, preparing to check the outside of the house to make sure no one was lurking about, when he noticed an envelope on the table beside him with his name on it.

His long fingers reached out for it and carefully began to open it. He glanced over at her to make sure she was still asleep because he wasn't sure what to expect and didn't want her looking at him or his reaction to whatever it was she'd felt the need to write to him about.

Remy,

First, I want to say to you that I'm sorry. Sorry for the way things have turned out, sorry that you sacrificed yourself to save me, and sorry for the way I've been acting. I do love you. I would say more than you can possibly know, but I think you know exactly how much I love you, because I know in my heart that you feel as strongly about me as I do you. Probably more so if what you've told me is true about how strongly vampires feel emotion. So, let me explain what is going on with me and where I'm at in my head. It'll be easier this way because otherwise, you'll interrupt me, then I'll get pissed, it'll disintegrate into an argument, and I don't want that. Stop laughing; you know that's exactly what would happen

She knew him too well. He *was* laughing, and she was spot on in her assessment. He continued reading.

When I thought you died, devastated was an understatement of how I felt. Seeing your lifeless body lying on a cold floor, knowing in my heart that you were gone, destroyed me. You were the last person I ever wanted to fall in love with, but once it happened, I couldn't imagine my life without you. I wanted to die just so I might have the chance to find you in whatever awaits us after death, and if there was nothing, well, then, at least I didn't have to feel the pain anymore.

When I think back to the amount of time I mourned you, it seemed like an eternity even though it was only a few hours. By the time I came back, you weren't dead, but you weren't you either. A cold, heartless thing had replaced the beautiful man I'd fallen in love with. The last thing I wanted to do was give up on you. I wanted to fix you, to make you see me and the love we shared again.

But every time I tried, you shot me down, claiming I was naïve or silly for wanting to try, but I didn't give up. You decided to send me away to live with Mary, and in a moment of weakness, I gave in to you. I wanted to feel you inside of me and reconnect on a level only we could reach together. In order to not feel so guilty and like I was cheating on you, I told you to lie to me, to pretend like you still loved me, and you did. You lied so well that I believed it was really you and that you had returned to me, but in an instant, your eyes were dark and cold again. You were gone.

I had these experiences with you several times over the past few months. I craved you and the only way I could find you was to request that you lie to me. You got so good at it, and in those moments, I was in heaven... Until we were finished and you brushed me off like I meant nothing.

This wore me down to the point where I had to give it up. I had to focus on finding my family instead of working on you because you were gone. It was only after Mary had figured out that you were possessed by Nicas that I began to have hope for us again. When I saw you look at the necklace, I watched your eyes grow warmer and brighter. I knew in my heart that it was you, but how long would it last? Nicas is still in you somewhere. So you see, when you came back to me last night, I couldn't allow myself to believe. I expected him to return and knock me flat on my ass again.

I still expect to look at you and see the cold eyes of a monster staring back at me, and I'm sorry for that. I want this to be real. I don't want it to be a lie. I want this to be us again, but I can't fully give myself to you until I'm sure.

135

Let's work together to find Mary so she can get rid of that evil bastard permanently. Once we accomplish that, we'll be free to be together again. I love you. You have to know that no matter what happens to me or us, you were the love of my life. Sound familiar? You once said those words to me, and I want you to know that no truer words have ever been spoken.

Love,

Sabine

Clutching the letter to his chest, his heart physically ached when he thought of all she had been through. Though he could remember glimpses of what she was talking about, her letter allowed him a deeper view into everything that had happened when he was in the darkness.

When he looked at her, the overwhelming feeling of love washed over him. He reached out to touch her soft skin, careful not to wake her. Leaning over her, he bent down and gently brushed his lips against hers. He wanted to take her, to claim her as his once again, but he'd respect her wishes to wait until a time when she could be sure that it was truly him and not Nicas. The thought of Nicas having his way with her body made him sick. *How was it that I was able to come through at those times? Why would he allow me to? Maybe he wasn't as strong as I was when it came to her. I can't imagine that I would ever sit back and allow someone to violate her. Maybe I sensed what was going on and fought my way back to her, but why couldn't I or didn't I tell her it truly was me? Nicas had to have still had his claws in me, controlling me. He was only able to convince her because he'd allowed me to take over... like a puppeteer.*

Does he still control me, and I'm oblivious? I know what I have to do.

* * *

The smell of bacon wafted through the air, rousing her awake. Her mouth watered in anticipation of the first bite. *Where is that smell coming from?*

Sabine opened her eyes, not knowing what to expect. Would he be there? Did he read the letter? Was the bacon within reach? A small tray holding a plate of food—bacon with a cheese omelet and a cup of hot tea—along with a handwritten letter sat on the bed beside her.

Which one first, the food or the letter? Sabine picked up the fork and the letter, looking at them both. Deciding to quiet her stomach first, she put the letter down and inhaled the food within minutes as she eyeballed the folded-up paper. Her shaking hand reached for the letter once more, and she began to read it.

To Sabine, my love,

I read the letter you left me, and I just want you to know that it has helped me to understand so much more than I did before. I don't have vivid memories of the last few months, only flashes... save for the times we made love. I don't know for sure why it is that he allowed me to come through at those times. I suspect he underestimated me and how hard I would fight to keep you safe from him, though he must have held some degree of control over me then, too.

Truth be told, I fear that he may still have control over me now, and it terrifies me beyond belief. I want nothing more than to be with you again, and I look forward to a time when our lives settle down a bit so we can reconnect. But that time is not now... Not while this other entity lurks inside me.

I won't put you in any more danger for now, and I plan to stay away until this is resolved. It's the only way I can ensure that you know whether it is him or me. As long as I am in control, you will not see me.

I'm sorry it has to be this way, but I cannot put your life in jeopardy any longer. I have someone watching your house at all times, so please don't feel as if I have abandoned you. I promise I will work day and night until I have Mary back.

Never in my life have I loved someone as much as I love you. I cannot fathom eternity without you and the thought of losing you someday, even if it is eighty years from now, makes me sick inside. Promise me that when this is all over with, you'll consider letting me turn you. I don't know if you know this, but there is such a thing in the vampire world as a mate (and no, I don't mean a friend, as you have undoubtedly heard me use the word mate that way before). A mate is one who is equal in all aspects to the one who makes them. My abilities and strengths would be your abilities and strengths. The love between mates intensifies drastically, and they long for no one else. They can feed almost exclusively from one another, only having to take human or animal blood occasionally. Most vampires scoff at the thought of taking a mate, but I can't think of anything that would mean

*more to me than spending eternity with you by my side.
Please, consider it, but know that no matter your
decision, I will be by your side, love.*

*I love you. I hope to have you in my arms once again
very soon...*

Love,

Remy

Warm, wet tears began to pool at the corners of her
eyes. She read the letter three more times before it could
truly sink in. How long would this ordeal last, and how
long would it be before they could be together again?
And would she choose a life of immortality for him?

CHAPTER 15

Mary raised her hands to her head and rubbed her throbbing temples. A piece of cloth covered her eyes tightly, but there was no mistaking the acrid scent of her mother's magic permeating the air around her.

"Mother? I know it's you."

She waited for a response, but she received none.

"Even after all these years, I still recognize your scent… Why the hell are you doing this to me?"

The cloth was yanked away from her face as a cold hand grasped her cheek. "We have bigger plans for you than training her to be his magic whore. I need your magic, and hers, to carry out our plan."

Her eyes adjusted, only to see who was holding her face. "Gretchen," she gasped.

"Not quite, my darling… not quite."

* * *

Damen lurked in the shadows around the house. Sensing the presence of another vampire inside, he stilled himself. Chances were high that the other vampire could sense him as well, unless he or she was newly changed. More than likely, the vampire inside wasn't more than a few months old and would be clueless to his presence. Since the fiasco of Remy killing Nicas, they hadn't heard from any other vampires who had been unaffected.

Sneaking closer to the house, he made one quick jump and landed with a soft thud on the roof. He crouched down and listened to the voice inside.

"She's not here. Doesn't look like she's been back... I swear, she never came out. The only one I saw come out was his progeny... Maybe he's taken her back to Willow Creek... Yeah... I'll go and let you know what I find..."

The vampire left the house and got into a car parked nearby. Damen instantly recognized him as Brendon, the same one who had been locked up for hurting Sabine... the same one who'd disappeared when Bastian did.

Damen pulled his phone out of his pocket and texted Remy before jumping down to follow Brendon on his Harley.

Brendon was here. He's on his way to Willow Creek. He must be working with Gretchen and Bastian.

A few moments later, a reply came through.

Don't engage him just yet. Follow him and see if he meets up with anyone. He's the best way for us to find out where they've taken Mary. I'll deal with him once he gets here.

Damen followed behind, careful to stay far enough back so he wouldn't be detected. As he neared the end of the street, the car Brendon drove pulled off into an empty parking space. Damen slowed the bike and contemplated what to do. If he kept going, he might lose sight of him, but if he stopped now, Brendon might notice him. Thinking quickly, he turned the bike down a side street where he could cut up an alley and get a glimpse of what Brendon was up to.

As he turned the bike, it halted suddenly, throwing him several feet before landing hard on his back. Tremendous pressure built in his head as his bones felt like they were breaking over and over again, rendering him paralyzed by pain. His sight went blurry, and he could hear nothing but a loud whooshing of air through his ears. A soft, sweet voice penetrated the noise.

"Damen… How easily we were able to lure you out. I'm sorry to have to hurt you like that, but Remy needs to know that he won't find us until we are ready to be found. It's only a matter of time before we have her. He might as well give her up now. Tell him I said hello, will you?"

Damen blinked, clearing his vision just long enough to see Gretchen, with her blonde hair pulled back high on her head, sauntering away with Mary by her side. His skull cracked one last time as he lost consciousness.

* * *

Sabine lay on her bed, staring at the ceiling. It had only been a few hours since she'd read Remy's letter, but she felt like she'd been without him for weeks. Just when she thought maybe she had really gotten him back, he was gone again.

I understand, but it still sucks. He's right, though. It probably is for the best. And, as usual, my mere existence puts me in danger because of my connection to him. It's pretty fucking sad that I'm finally home, yet I can't even enjoy it. Maybe I should *become a vampire, so I won't always be so vulnerable. Not sure I can get on board with the whole blood diet thing, though. Yuck.*

She sat up just in time to see the air distort in the corner of the room. Sabine stiffened in anticipation. If Remy was appearing to her already, then Nicas was back, and as much as she wanted to see him, she didn't want him under that circumstance.

A form began to appear, but it wasn't Remy. The telltale curves of a woman moved from the corner into the light.

"How are you, Sabine?"

"Gretchen, what are you doing here? I've missed you! I've wanted to talk to you about some things." She knew Gretchen had taken Mary, but if she played dumb, maybe she could get some information out of her before help came. Someone had to be just outside and within earshot. Thankfully, the bracelet Mary had given her to shield her thoughts was still firmly around her wrist. Otherwise, playing dumb wouldn't have been so easy.

"Oh, and what would those things be?" She looked at Sabine coolly.

"The way I acted the day I thought Remy died. I shouldn't have been such a bitch to you."

"Water under the bridge." Gretchen waved her hand and looked around the room. "I don't even really remember it, to tell you the truth."

"Glad that's cleared up, but why are you here?"

Gretchen smirked. "Hmm... you're leverage, of course. At least that's how he will see it, not knowing that the magic within you is the real reason we need you."

"But, I haven't tapped into it... It's useless to take me for that reason."

"You have accessed it. Mary has already told us you did."

"Only once."

"If you did it once, you can do it again," Gretchen moved closer to Sabine, placing her hand on her shoulder. "Close your eyes, dear. This might make you a little dizzy."

A scream erupted from Sabine's throat, but it was extinguished within a second by a backhand from Gretchen. She fell to her butt, cracking her head on the leg of her vanity table chair. Gretchen was on her, and Sabine kicked and punched at her as best she could. She tried hard to tap into her magic. Nothing but a flicker was all she could muster. It was nowhere near enough to subdue Gretchen.

She was yanked from the floor as she started to lose consciousness from the blow to her head. The room began to shimmer as she was whisked away.

CHAPTER 16

He'd been making rounds in the neighborhood, making sure no one out of the ordinary was lurking about, when he heard a split-second scream. Racing back up the street, he exploded into Sabine's room, only to find it empty.

He dropped to his knees. *I've failed her. I brought her here to be safe, and Gretchen got to her anyway.* A fiery sensation churned deep within him. Standing, he picked up a chair and launched it across the room, shattering the mirror on the vanity table. Stepping in front of the broken and cracked shards that still remained, he watched as his own eyes darkened, pulling him back into nothingness.

* * *

Sabine rubbed her face, still stinging from the impact of Gretchen's hand. A familiar voice echoed in the background as she regained consciousness.

"She's awake..."

Blinking, she could make out someone who looked a lot like Mary sitting next to her.

Gretchen moved swiftly across the room and took her hand, "I'm sorry for that. I had to make it convincing in case he was listening. I really didn't want to hurt you, but the more believable, the better."

"I don't believe that for a second. Why say you needed me for my magic if you thought he was listening?

"Because he didn't believe you had tapped into it. I wanted to make him think we would fail if we tried to use you."

"Why are you acting buddy/buddy with her, Mary? She kidnapped you just like she did me, and for what? All to get back at Remy?"

Mary pursed her lips together as she took a deep breath. Exhaling, she began to speak. "A lot has happened, and you need to trust me. She had to take you, and me, because we never would have listened otherwise. They mean to take out Nicas by any means necessary, and it had to look believable to catch him by surprise when we attack. That's why they took us instead of asking us to join."

"Wait... They?"

"Yes, I know this looks like Gretchen, but my mother has taken over her body for the time being and Bastian is here, too."

"But you hate both of them..."

"Things change under the right circumstances. They still aren't my favorite people in the world, but I believe in what they're trying to do, and I think you should, too."

"Where is Bastian? I want to talk to him."

"Just in the next room. Go to him."

She stood, making her way into the other room. Bastian sat at a table, deep in thought, while Brendon sat slouching in the chair next to him like he was bored to death. She clutched her stomach at the sight of the one who had hurt her for days just because he could. As good as a vampire bite could feel, it could be equally as bad if the vampire didn't take the pain away. Brendon had taken pleasure in making it so she couldn't even scream when he ripped into her flesh.

"Do not be afraid. Brendon will not harm you. I have made sure of it. As his maker, I have commanded him to leave you alone."

"I want to leave. This was weird two seconds ago, and it's even worse now. Why is *he* here? Why are *you* here? Why is Gretchen possessed by Kristine?"

"So many questions, and I assure you, I have the answers. Sit down. Brendon will leave if it makes you more comfortable."

"Yeah, I think that's for the best." She eyed him nervously. She didn't trust that he wouldn't hurt her. He was a sadistic lunatic, and she briefly wondered if he was capable of disobeying Bastian because of it. Hell, she didn't trust that Bastian wouldn't hurt her either now that he was apparently a vampire again.

"Brendon proved crucial in helping me escape. That is the only reason he is still here. I do not care for him at all, but sometimes, one needs a general lackey, and he has played the role well. Kristine originally took possession of Brendon's body when she broke me out of that cell, and we soon happened upon Gretchen by chance. You see, Gretchen was more than willing to help our cause after the way she had been treated. Once Kristine explained to her that Nicas had taken over

Remington's mind and body, she understood it was for the best to let Kristine inhabit her in order to save him."

"How did you know it was Nicas way back then? It took us awhile to figure it out."

"One does not forget what the presence of their maker feels like. Even as a human, it was unmistakable. Oh, but he was clever enough to coerce me into not telling anyone. Luckily for me, Kristine had been watching everything that transpired. She was able to explain to Gretchen through Brendon without me. That is when Gretchen offered to turn me once more."

"So, you're a vampire again. I don't know whether to be happy for you or pissed that you got what you wanted. What's your end game here?"

"To rid the world of Nicas, once and for all. He is far too powerful and too far gone to coexist with the rest of civilization. It will only be a matter of time before he desires to rule the world. It was that same desire that caused him to seek out immortality and vampirism in the first place."

"If you get rid of him, won't that make you human again?"

"If it does, so be it. I cannot sit back and let Remy rot inside himself, even after the differences we had. He deserves to be set free. What kind of maker would I be if I didn't try and help him?"

"But you aren't his maker anymore."

"Perhaps not, but he is still a son to me. I cannot throw away centuries of memories with him."

"I don't get it. You beat him nearly to death and locked him away, yet you don't think it's right for him to be possessed by Nicas? The only explanation I have is that all you vampires are mental."

Bastian chuckled. "I know it is hard to understand from a human perspective, but when you are immortal, grievances happen that can last many years, yet we always make up in the end because we have an eternity to overcome our issues. Though we act as savages at time, we are still family."

"Speaking of family, would you mind telling me just what the hell you did with mine?"

"I did nothing with them."

"Cut the bullshit. I know you told them and my friends that I was dead."

"I simply convinced them to leave town. Nothing more. I did not tell them where to go, and I do not know where they currently are."

"You think making my parents believe I was dead is nothing?"

Bastian looked away for just a second before meeting her gaze again. "I understand this upsets you, but you have to realize that it was easier all around for familial ties of the chosen ones to be severed."

She shook her head defiantly. "No, it wasn't better. I thought everyone abandoned me, but then I guess that's what you wanted, right? It was easier for you if we were good little prisoners who didn't try to keep contact with the outside world."

Bastian was silent. "I will make it up to you somehow. This, I promise."

"What about all the others before me? Hm?

"I do not care about the others. I know you do not want to believe it, but I do care about you. It saddens me that you are so angry with me. It was a mistake on my part. I only wish to see you happy."

There it was. He still wanted her even after everything that had happened. The thought of it sickened her, and she began to wonder if his plan was more about taking her for his own again than saving Remy.

"Oh, I'm angry for sure, but I also think you're full of it. You don't know anything about me to truly care about me." Sabine glared at him for what seemed like an eternity before something occurred to her that might clue her in to his true intentions.

"Wait a minute, when you say you want to rid the world of Nicas, and earlier, they said by any means necessary, you don't mean Remy will be harmed in the process do you?"

Bastian rubbed his chin as he looked at her. "Though I will do everything in my power to ensure he comes out of this unharmed because I owe it to him for trying to claim you and locking him away, it is a possibility. I must confess that I do not know what will happen once Nicas is expelled. Remy could be fine, but he might go along with him."

"No! Just go to him and tell him you want to help. He'll let you. I know he will. There is no need to put him in any danger."

"Remy is not himself. I do not expect cooperation from him."

"You don't understand. He is himself! I swear he is. When Gretchen took Mary, I triggered something in him in the basement, and he came back."

"Can you say absolutely that it is him?"

Sabine settled back in her chair. Her silence was all the answer Bastian needed.

Working with Bastian was the last thing she wanted to do, but it seemed like her only option. "What's the plan?" she asked hesitantly.

* * *

He sat quietly in the ballroom. The mansion was empty, and he found himself alone, wondering what the next move would be. Though Remy had proved to be strong, Nicas had found a weak moment and overtook him easily enough.

What was Gretchen planning? He'd heard just enough to gather that Sabine was going to be used against him, either for leverage or for a spell they were concocting. *Stupid move. I could not care less about that girl. Her blood was divine, but I'll find another to replace her. I suspect my desire for her was only a side effect of Remington trying to find his way out.*

Damen came racing into the room, almost startling him.

"You have no idea what kind of crap I've had to deal with."

"I don't really care either."

"You better care because they're coming for you."

"Who?"

"Mary and Gretchen. They kicked my ass and told me to tell you that you wouldn't see them until they were ready for you, and that you should just hand over Sabine to them now."

"They've already taken her." He laughed uncontrollably for a few minutes before regaining his composure. "They are no match for me. A new vampire and a witch? They'd be stupid to try me." His eyes rose to meet Damen's.

"Nicas?"

"Just now figuring it out?"

"No, but Remy was in control when I last saw you."

"Well, he isn't now, is he? Let them come. I'll take great pleasure in exterminating them."

"Can I leave now?"

"Why? You don't want to miss out on the fun, do you?"

"Well, let's see, I've had every bone in my body broken over and over by them just because you are technically my maker, even though you really aren't, and I've spent the last day trying to heal. No, I'd rather not see them again… or you. I'm just lucky that while they were snapping my neck numerous times in succession, they didn't completely sever my head."

"It does not matter what body I am in because I *am* your maker and the maker of all vampires. You can go, but only after you do one more thing for me… Fetch Sam and bring her to me."

"No… I won't bring her into this mess." He tried hard not to think about how the shifter girl made him feel, fearing Nicas would use it against him.

"*You will. Go now and bring her back.* She means a great deal to both Mary and Sabine, and I need her."

Damen ran into the woods, stopping in the middle of a clearing. The pain began to set in the moment he disobeyed Nicas' order to bring Sam back. He wouldn't do it, and there was only one thing that could at least temporarily stop him. In one swift motion, he reached up to his head and chin, breaking his own neck. It would buy her some time before he woke up again.

CHAPTER 17

A peaceful calmness settled over the town of Willow Creek. People moved about in their homes and around the small community as if it were any other day, not knowing that all hell was about to break loose at the mansion high up on the hill.

The faintest sound of footsteps alerted him to their presence. He could hear them inching closer, trying to be quieter than mice. He waited patiently for them upon his throne in the ballroom, where he'd been perched for hours. Wanting to be where they could easily find him and he could easily detect them when they arrived, the ballroom seemed like the best choice.

At once, the doors swung open, and the whole lot of them entered. Standing elbow to elbow, they formed a line in front of him.

Bastian stepped forward and cleared his throat. "You will leave this place now. If you do not, we will be forced to act."

Nicas chuckled and threw his hand up as if he were about to swat a gnat pretending to be a hornet away. "You can try."

"We will do more than try."

"Oh, and how is that? Three new vampires, a witch, and a wannabe witch who leans closer to human? I'd love to see you try. I could really go for a little entertainment. You know, this town really is a boring place. I shall be leaving as soon as I'm through with you."

Nicas leapt through the air, but hit an invisible wall of magic ten feet in front of them and was flung backwards until the far wall broke his trajectory. He stood, glaring at them. Pacing back and forth, he contemplated about who he should try and take out first. Sabine would be the easiest. She hadn't yet tapped into any real power within, at least not enough to stop him. Next would come Mary, then Gretchen and Brendon, and finally, he would take his time torturing Bastian for as long as it still brought him some minute amount of joy.

Walking carefully to the point where the magical barrier began, he carefully sent out a jolt of power, dismantling it easily enough. An evil grin spread across his face as he made his way to Sabine.

Sabine stood with her chin held high, smiling at him.

"What are you so happy about? I'm going to kill you first, but not before I have one last taste of you." His fangs descended, gleaming under the lights of the ballroom. "Should I lie to you first?"

"You won't have to, because Remy will be here soon enough."

"I doubt that. You see, all that time he was able to keep me at bay, I was quietly building and storing my strength. He doesn't have a hope in the world of overtaking me now."

"Maybe something *out* of this world will do the trick."

Sabine looked at Mary and nodded. Mary's eyes darkened, and she began chanting an incantation.

Gretchen, or rather Kristine, took her hand and joined in the chant, gathering power with every word. Heat rose in the room as the air became thick around them.

Nicas moved forward slowly. His legs were heavy, like he was walking in quicksand. He managed to inch closer to Sabine, and just as he was about to reach out and grab her, she took Mary's other hand.

The force of the three of them chanting slammed into him, knocking him to the floor. Struggling to stand again, he couldn't get any higher than his knees before falling back once more. The lights flickered as the room darkened. A flash of fire from the corner of the room caught his eye.

A dark mass emerged through the fire and floated toward him. The smell of sulfur assaulted his nose as the form began to shimmer and take shape. Before his eyes, a woman with grey skin, wearing tight red clothing, appeared.

"Nicas, my lover, my, how you've changed… I quite miss the way you used to look, but this body suits you."

"Why are you here?" He glanced away from her as he tried to scoot backward. "We had a deal, remember? You leave me alone as long as I still live."

"I remember quite well, but the fact of the matter is, you died. Had it not been for these three lovely women alerting me to your presence here just now, I might have missed that little detail. You belong to me now."

"I didn't die. I merely took over another body."

"There are no loopholes when dealing with demons and the agreements you make with them. I granted you immortality so long as your soul became mine to add to my collection *if* you ever managed to be killed. Your spinal cord was severed completely in two, and you belong to me now."

"You can't take me. I'm too powerful." Nicas stood defiantly.

A sultry giggle emanated from the demoness. "This is going to be fun." She sauntered over to Nicas and placed her hands on his face before he could muster the speed to run away.

"Wait!" Sabine screamed. "What will happen to Remy?"

The demoness turned, a red flicker dancing in her eyes. "Someone must be sacrificed for summoning me. Might as well be him since the two are entangled. I can take him to the other side and drop him on my way back to hell with this one."

"No, please!" Sabine fell to her knees, begging for Remy to be spared. "Don't take him."

She looked at Sabine with a hint of sympathy on her face. "I'm sorry, sweet girl. These are the rules we must play by." Nicas squirmed in her grip as she spoke.

Bastian placed his hand on Sabine's shoulder. "Take me instead," he said, stepping forward.

Kristine, in the form of Gretchen, gasped in unison with Sabine. "No! We were going to make a life together now that I'm back. You can't do this to me... You are the reason I still exist."

"So that was your plan all along, Mother?" Mary asked. "You stole Gretchen's body so you could come back for Bastian. You're no better than the filth taking up space inside Remy."

"I've been dead for a long time, dear. You'd do the same if you were in my shoes, with your true love within your grasp."

"Silence," the demoness hissed at the two bickering women. Turning back toward Bastian, she asked, "Why should I take you instead of the one within?"

"Because I have lived a long, full life. I have had plenty of time to do the things I wanted to do, and I chose to spend my years getting drunk on power as the lord of this town, destroying the lives of innocents every ten years just so I could be in control. No one will mourn me when I am gone. Taking Remington would destroy not only him, but Sabine as well. I have been in the world for over fourteen hundred years, the majority of those as vampire, yet here I am, a newborn vampire again. The power I have now pales in comparison to what I had before when I channeled Nicas' power. I know I will never again attain that, nor do I want to... Take me. I am tired of this life, and I am ready to move on to the next," He turned to Kristine, "I will see you there, my darling."

"Come to me," the demoness summoned. He moved closer to her as she placed her hand on his face. The air shimmered as a flame began to lick the air. A flash of light blazed, leaving two unmoving bodies lying on the floor in its wake.

Kristine screamed and dropped to the floor as she left Gretchen's body.

Sabine scrambled over to Remy, placing her arms around him as best she could. Through tears, she begged. "Please, please... Come back to me. I can't lose you again. I know you can hear me. Come back to me..."

Brendon took a quiet step back, trying to make an exit, when he ran into Damen, who had come in, without Sam, on the tail end of the confrontation. Once Nicas had been slowed, the command began to weaken and he was able to return to the Manor. "Not so fast, buddy. I'm pretty sure they're going to want to deal with you sooner or later."

"But I helped! Let me go! I won't bother any of you again, I swear."

"Nope..." Damen pushed him forward and kept a tight hold on Brendon's arm.

Mary got down on her knees and held Gretchen's hand as her eyes fluttered open. "Welcome back, honey."

"Did it work? Is Remy safe?"

"It worked, but Remy..." she said, shaking her head somberly, tears streaking down her face.

Sabine rocked with Remy's body in her arms. He was cold and lifeless and all she could think to do was to put her wrist against his mouth, urging him to feed. She didn't care if it hurt. She only cared that it might bring him back to her. She couldn't lose him again.

CHAPTER 18

The events of the previous few minutes played in front of his eyes like a dream. A tremendous pressure had been lifted from him when the demoness placed her hands upon his face. The darkness quickly faded away, and the sweet call of nothingness beckoned to him. How easy it would be to just stop, to just sleep forever and find peace.

Through the distance, a voice called to him. His skin moistened with warm tears as something pressed against his mouth. The voice was sweet and familiar... *Sabine. I can hear you, love.*

* * *

When he didn't open his mouth to take her wrist, she laid her head on his chest, sobbing until she could cry no more. Mary patted Sabine's back while the others gathered around. She lifted her head, looking up at Mary, and threw her arms around the witch.

"Shhh, honey. Maybe it's just gonna take time for him to wake up... You did an excellent job helping with the summoning, you know? If it weren't for you, I don't know that we would have had enough power to summon her."

Sabine nodded. "I know," she whispered.

"Look!" Damen said abruptly, pointing at Remy. "His face just moved."

"I was looking right him, and I didn't see anything. Don't get her hopes up," Mary said.

"I'm not getting her hopes up. His face moved."

Sabine turned and stared at him, willing him to move again if he truly had moved in the first place. She turned to Damen and asked, "Is his heart still beating?"

"Barely."

Just then, cool fingers grasped Sabine's hand, pulling her close. When she turned toward him, Remy's eyes fluttered but didn't open all the way.

"Open your eyes for me, please? Please! Open your eyes!" Sabine didn't know whether to cry or laugh, so she did both. "Come back to me," she whispered.

The corner of his mouth eased up into a half smile. "I couldn't stay away from you, love."

She collapsed onto him as the air left her body while she momentarily forgot how to breathe. *Everything is going to be okay...*

Brendon scoffed and tried to wiggle his way out of Damen's grip. "Now that everything is wonderful, I'll just get out of here and leave you all alone."

Sabine scrambled to her feet and marched toward Brendon. "I'm going to kill you, you sick son of a bitch! I won't let you hurt anyone else like you did me. Bastian never should have turned you again. He should have killed you when he had the chance."

During the brief amount of time she'd spent with Mary and Kristine preparing for the spell, they'd helped her learn to use emotion to her advantage when she wanted to tap into the magic within. This would be the best use of it she could think of. Raising her hand, she sent a blast of pure hatred aimed straight toward his neck in the hopes of breaking it over and over again until his spinal cord would finally snap, effectively severing his head.

A hand gripped her wrist, turning her away from Brendon. She looked up into the emerald green eyes of Remy as he held her in place.

"Stop, love. You never get over the first kill. Don't let him haunt you for the rest of your life. This isn't you..." he said, embracing her, "but, it is me."

Within a second, Remy let go of her and leapt at Brendon, grasping the young vampire's head and tearing it away from his body before he knew what hit him.

Tossing Brendon's head aside, he looked down at his bloodied hands and disappeared from the ballroom. Sabine ran after him, leaving the others behind. She went to the first place she could think of that he might go. She hurried back to the room they had shared and into the library.

He stood quietly, looking through the bay window. She walked over to him and placed her hands on his chest, hugging him from behind.

His head fell forward as his hands overlapped hers. He relished the warmth of her body against his.

"Sabine, I want you to go home for a while."

"I don't want to leave you now that we can finally be together."

"I have a lot to process since Nicas was stripped away. I don't know what abilities I still have. I can barely remember anything that's happened or the things I've done. I need some space, just for a few days, to clear my head. Can you give me that?"

"I can... but, I want you to kiss me before I go."

He turned to her, placing his forehead against hers, and closed his eyes as he breathed her in.

"I've missed your lips, love." His hands, still bloodied, caressed her jawline, just below her ears.

She placed her hands on either side of his neck and pulled him closer. His lips feathered across hers as her knees went weak. For the first time in months, she knew unquestionably that he had returned to her and that this wasn't a cruel joke Nicas was playing on her. Every trial and tribulation they'd been through had all been worth it because it led them to the place they were in at that moment.

His lips pushed harder against her as his tongue searched for hers. She pressed her body against him, trying to close the smallest amount of space between them. Against her lips, he said, "I am so hungry," before kissing her deeper. "It's been weeks..."

"Let me feed you," she replied breathlessly.

His power washed over her in an instant, threatening to knock her already weakened legs out from underneath her. Steadying her in his arms, he sunk his teeth deep into her throat, relishing her taste. The bitterness was gone, and the sweetness that remained tickled his throat. His nails dug into her shoulder, causing her to whimper, but not from pain. Every touch, every caress, every motion threatened to undo her.

She began to go lightheaded and the sound of her heart slowing pulled him back to reality.

"Are you okay? I think I took too much, love. I couldn't help myself."

She smiled up at him, her eyes sleepily staring through hooded lids. "I feel fantastic."

"I think you need to lie down." He picked her up and carried her to the bedroom, placing her on the bed. "Rest for a bit before you go home. I have some things I must do, and the sooner I can do them, the better." Pulling the bedspread up over her, he pricked his finger with his fang and rubbed the two puncture wounds on her neck. They closed up instantly as she drifted off to sleep.

He went into the bathroom and fetched a washcloth that he ran under the hot water. Returning to her, he wiped the warm cloth against her neck and sides of her face to clean up the blood he'd left behind. Once she was clean, he tossed the washcloth back into the bathroom and turned to leave.

Closing the door behind him, he listened for voices. Once he'd locked onto Mary's voice, he headed in her direction. Finding her outside the Manor in the cool autumn air talking on her cell phone, he approached her cautiously and waited for her to finish her conversation. Mary had always been a friend, yet he couldn't help but feel terrible that he'd pulled her into the latest drama in

Willow Creek. If she felt like ripping him a new one for it, he would have felt like he deserved it.

"Mary, I don't know how I can ever thank you for everything you've done."

"No need... I know the asshole wasn't you this time, and I would do it over again to help that girl up there. Destiny has not been her friend, has she?"

"No, though I don't mind that destiny chose to stick her with me."

"You really do love her... I wasn't always sure. When you get angry with her over the little things, just remember the hell she went through for you."

"I'll never forget it, even if she isn't mine anymore."

"Oh, this shit again, huh? She loves you. There is no need in the world to throw that away."

"I only meant that she is no longer forced to be paired with me, but just look how much danger she has been in since she met me."

"She's shaping up to be a good witch, and a good witch is a safe witch. She's learned to use her emotions as power, and that can be the greatest source of magic there is. She won't always need you to protect her, though I'm sure she won't mind it now and then."

"I can't help but think how normal her life can be. It's a matter of time before she's reunited with her family, she's still a talented artist, and I still have the means to take care of her for the rest of her life. I'm just not sure having me in her life is what's best for her."

"Here's a thought, jackass... Let her make that decision for herself. If she chooses to go on without you, then so be it, but don't take the choice away from her. All that will do is show her that *you* don't want to be with her."

"I want her more than anything."

"Then just stop. Be happy for once. You've earned it after four hundred years, you know..."

He tried hard to hide the smile that was quickly taking place on his lips, but he wasn't fast enough for Mary not to see it and smirk to herself.

"So what's next for you?" Remy asked.

"Home... alone. I'm looking forward to the quiet. I loved having Sabine there and Sam before that, but I've learned to love my private time, too."

"Have you heard from Sam?"

Mary nodded. "Yeah, she and her mother are looking forward to seeing Sabine again. It's been quite a while."

"They're neighbors now."

"Oh, yeah?"

"Sam lives just a block down the street from Sabine."

"Thanks to you."

"Thanks to Sabine. It was her suggestion to buy them a home. That happened when Nicas was mostly in control, but I actually do remember that she is what got the ball rolling, and I ran with it when I was able to."

"You're a good man, Remy... even if you are a fucking vampire." Mary reached out and embraced Remy.

"There is one more thing I could really use some help with before you leave, if you don't mind."

"Always wanting something from this old gal. Some things never change. What is it?"

"Destroy the spell on this town. I don't want to rule over it, and the agreement was bound in magic."

"But everyone will be able to tell whomever they please that vampires exist. Are you ready for that?"

"I don't care anymore. I'm not concerned about a lynch mob coming after me, and even if they did, I'm pretty sure I could take them," he said, sounding like his normally cocky self. "I'm quite a bit more powerful than I used to be, in case you hadn't noticed."

She reached up and patted him on the cheek as she smiled. "I'll do it."

* * *

"Gretchen, can I speak to you?" Remy had left Mary alone with the document to work her magic on undoing it. He planned to meet with the mayor of Willow Creek the next day to tell him of the news. Sabine would be happy, knowing that no other youth would ever again have to be sacrificed. He longed to leave Willow Creek and return to New York or London, but if she chose to stay there and wanted to be with him, then he would never leave her.

"Of course," she said, running her fingers through her blonde hair. "How are you holding up?"

"It is me who should be asking you that question. I'm sorry for the way I acted."

"It wasn't you. I know that now. I have no hard feelings toward you... brother. May I call you that again?"

"I'd like nothing more than for you to call me that, sister. Is it true that Bastian sacrificed himself for me?"

"It is, the old fool. Old fool for getting us all into this situation in the first place, not old fool for saving you." Her eyes misted over with red tears that threatened to stain her perfectly made-up cheeks at any moment. "I do miss him so much already. I know he could be a hard ass, but he's what I've known for so long."

"You still have me."

"I do, but you'll be starting your life with Sabine, and you need time alone with her. I think I'll do a bit of traveling. It's been ages since I visited Moscow. I think I'll go there first.

"I hope you have a wonderful time... Could you take Sabine home for me?"

"That depends... Does she want to go home? I have no desire to incur her wrath if you're making her do something she doesn't want to do. She was fairly rude to me when you sent me to fetch her, you know? It's a good thing I don't hold grudges." Gretchen chuckled.

"She'll be happy once she gets there. I promise. I spoke to her friend earlier, and she has been helping me set up something pretty special. It's been a few hours now, so it should be all good to go. Let me talk to her first."

Remy took off as fast he could to Sabine. She still slept, quietly snoring, on the bed as he gently shook her.

"It's time to go home, love." He watched as the sleep faded from her eyes, and she turned on her side toward him.

"I don't want to go."

"You have to. Lana is waiting for you, and I promised you'd be there shortly."

"When will I see you again?"

"In a few days... but I have something to discuss with you before you go."

She sat up, rubbing her eyes and yawning. "What's up?"

"I don't know how to say this, so I'm just going to come out with it. I'm giving you a few days to make a choice."

"What choice?"

"I want you to spend time at home really thinking about the life you want and where I fit into it... or don't."

"You're talking nonsense, Remy. I want you in my life. Period. No amount of thinking will change that."

"I know you say that now, but I want you to really think about it. I'm ready to go to the ends of the earth with you if that's what you choose, but I also want to give you the opportunity to return to the life you had before. I've got Mary working to undo the arrangement between this town and the vampires. There will be no more offerings and no more vampire population, save for me if you choose for us to stay here, and with Nicas gone, there will no longer be a supernatural pull to the area."

"That's really awesome of you. I'm so glad you're doing away with it. I know you've made some child very happy knowing they will never have to leave their family behind... But, what's the catch? You want me to ditch you, or choose to be a vampire, don't you?"

He glanced at the ceiling, not wanting to see the reaction she had when he answered her. "Yes, but I don't just want to turn you. I want you to be my mate, like I explained in the letter I wrote to you. What are your thoughts?"

"I want to spend the rest of my life with you... I'm just not sure how long I want that life to last. It's not that I don't want that time with you. I just need to think about the things I would be giving up... like pizza and wine." She smirked to lighten the mood a bit.

He looked back at her and ran his fingers through her dark hair. "Then I suggest you go and think on it. Lana will be leaving if you don't show up soon. Gretchen will take you whenever you're ready."

CHAPTER 19

The car ride to Sabine's house hadn't turned out as awkwardly as she'd thought. Gretchen was warm, friendly, and downright nice to her, though she wouldn't have blamed her had she acted like she hated Sabine. She'd profusely apologized once they were in the car since her last apology didn't really count. That had been Kristine, not Gretchen, she'd said sorry to.

As they pulled into the driveway, Gretchen reached into the console of the car and pulled out a set of keys. "Here... he said these are yours."

She grasped the keys and felt the coolness of the metal under her fingers. Home was the single best gift he could've given her. Too bad her family wasn't there to celebrate it, but it was all just a matter of time before she would find them again. At least she was getting her friends back. She couldn't wait to see Lana again, and Delia needed to know she wasn't dead, too. As soon as she could make it to New York or Delia came back to Willow Creek, they could make her see the truth as well.

"Thank you, Gretchen. Hope we can hang out again soon."

"Once I'm back in the States, it's a date."

She got out, closing the car door behind her, and jogged up the sidewalk to the front door. Putting the key in the lock, she turned it and went inside. Lana sat on the couch, and to her surprise, Sam and her mother joined her.

She threw her purse to the ground and ran to all three women, giving them a group hug and reveling in the fact that they were all in *her* home—safe, sound, and happy. Lana was the first to break the hug, pulling Sabine away from the other two women.

Barely able to contain herself, she exclaimed that there was another big surprise.

Sabine was confused because she had thought Sam and Samantha were her welcome-home surprise since she hadn't seen either one of them in months. She glanced over her shoulder as movement from the dining room caught her attention.

"Dad!" She ran into her father's arms, clutching him as if he might disappear on her if she let go. She screamed into his shoulder as tears of joy flowed down her face. "I missed you so much! Where is...?"

In an instant, her mother's face appeared behind her father. Sabine reached out, embracing her mother and inhaling the precious scent of her perfume. Another set of arms wrapped around her, and this time, they belonged to her sister, Shay.

"We saw you... dead," her mother sobbed. "I can't believe you're here."

"How are you here now?" Sabine asked, wiping tears from her and her mother's eyes.

"Lana got us to come back, and when we got here, Remy made us realize the truth. Truth be told, I thought *he* was the one who was crazy or that he was playing some kind of trick on us, but here you are..."

"Here I am, and the house is ours again!"

"We'll work all the details out soon enough, but let's just enjoy our time together right now," her father said.

* * *

Two days had gone by with her family under the same roof. No matter the distance and time that had separated them, nothing had really changed. She was thankful to have them back in her life. Unfortunately, they had started their lives over in Washington, Pennsylvania, which was not all that far from Willow Creek. Though she never wanted her family to leave again, they had to get back to their other house and her father's new job. Shay was enrolled in a private school with a strict attendance policy, and she couldn't afford to miss any classes if she hoped to get a good recommendation for college from the school's administrators.

They'd said their goodbyes earlier that morning, with promises made to speak every night either by phone or Skype and weekend visits planned as soon as possible. Sabine had barely had time to contemplate the decision laid out before her.

Flopping herself down on the couch, she wondered what exactly it would be like to crave blood instead of food. What would her family think? Would she scare them off after just getting them back, or would they be supportive of her decision? Did she really want to give up the opportunity to have children? She'd tried hard to convince herself that she didn't want kids. Mainly, because being chosen as the person to fulfill the agreement, she knew there was no way she could ever have the opportunity. What if this was her chance now?

Could I really spend eternity on this earth and never taste another cupcake or slice of pizza?

She loved Remy more than she ever thought possible, but was he enough to fulfill her for eternity? *Fuck if I know... Eternity is a long time.*

She laid in silence on the couch for over an hour debating. One minute, she'd have herself convinced that being a vampire wasn't such a bad thing, and then immediately talk herself into staying human. After all, if she stayed human, she could continue to practice magic, and that wasn't such a bad thing. But could she practice magic as a vampire? *Gretchen/Kristine had managed to do it, so it must be possible.*

"Not wearing your bracelet, are you?"

She gasped and shot up into a sitting position. "I hate when you do that!"

Remy leaned against the wall, flashing her a cocky grin. "I love getting a rise out of you, and you should be expecting it by now."

"Was I really thinking that loudly?"

"Yes. It was deafening. I could hear you clear outside."

"I don't know what I want..." she said, looking away from him.

"It's okay, love. If you need more time, then take more time." He stood, walking toward the front door.

"I'll come back when you're ready to give me an answer."

"Wait," she said, standing up. "I've decided."

"Are you sure?"

"Yes... First, I want to thank you for everything you've given me, everything you showed me during those months together in Europe. No words can express how truly grateful I am for those memories, and I will cherish them forever."

His shoulders relaxed and his head dipped. "But..."

She shook her head. "Just listen... You've given my family, my friends, and my life back to me." She walked closer to him, reaching up and brushing a loose stand of hair away from his face. "I love you, and I always will, no matter what... That's why I've decided..."

"It's okay, love. I'll leave you alone if that's what you want. Just let me take care of you. I can set up a bank account for you and you can stay here or even take my apartment in Manhattan..."

"Remy, just shut up." She stood on her tiptoes and kissed him, catching him off guard. He stumbled back a step before returning the kiss. "I want you now and forever. Make me yours."

He exhaled air he didn't need anyway against her lips in a show of disbelief. Scooping her into his arms, he took her to her bedroom and laid her down, briefly trying to explain the process.

"I don't care what the steps are, just do it."

His hand grazed her belly as his lips claimed her. She moaned softly into his mouth as his hand slid up under her shirt and bra, cupping her breast, thumb circling her nipple.

She pushed his shirt up over his head, running her fingers over his smooth body. He continued to kiss her as his hand toyed with the button of her jeans before undoing them. Moving quickly down to her feet, he yanked her jeans and panties off, throwing them aside.

Standing upright, he slowly unbuttoned his jeans, sliding them off. He pushed her thighs apart and buried his face in between them. His tongue glided over her as he sent a wave of power over her, preparing her for the bite to come.

His strong hands explored her soft curves as his tongue continued to stroke her. Kissing a trail up her body, he lingered at her breasts before moving up to kiss her neck. His cock pressed against her as a whimper of anticipation escaped her lips.

He looked down at her underneath him before plunging himself deep inside of her.

His green eyes brightened, fangs descending as he moved rhythmically in and out of her

"Do it," she whispered. "Make me your mate."

He opened his mouth wide and bit down on her neck. Her blood flowed into his mouth.

She went lightheaded as he took more and more of her blood, but she felt no pain. He sat back and pulled her up to him, lips never leaving her throat.

She went limp in his arms as the room began to darken. She could barely make out Remy reaching for his discarded jeans, taking out her Eiffel Tower charm from the pocket. He jammed the tip into his neck and placed her mouth over the wound.

His blood, warm and metallic tasting, flowed down her throat, almost gagging her at first. As she took more of his blood, it became sweeter until she began to crave it. Nothing else would ever quench the thirst that had overtaken her senses.

Remy pushed her to her back again and let loose the animalistic side of him. He fucked her harder than she'd ever been fucked as he passed his power and abilities to her through his blood, willing her to become his mate. She continued to drink from him until her body started to convulse. The strongest orgasm she'd ever experienced washed over her as the world and Remy faded away.

She lay still for a few moments, barely aware that he was still inside her. Blinking, she saw the world in a whole new way for the first time. Colors seemed more vibrant. Sounds were more amplified. Her love for him dialed itself up a notch or ten.

Remy smiled down at her and kissed her hard on the lips. With strength she never had before, she pushed him away, slamming him to his back on the bed. She straddled him, aching for them to become one once more.

Riding him, she moaned as she dipped her head and crashed her lips against his. He grabbed her hips hard, hanging onto her as she brought him damn near to orgasm.

Her gums ached as the taste of his blood still coated her mouth. Running her tongue over her teeth, two sharp points began to take form. The sweet release of her fangs caused the thirst to return, and she sank her teeth into his neck.

His body tensed before he flipped them back over and continued to pump into her. He plunged his fangs into her neck and slapped the mattress hard as he came inside of her.

Her center began to pulsate and tingle with intensity as she was pushed over the edge seconds later.

Remy collapsed on top of her, gently kissing her neck and cheek. "How do you feel?"

"I've never been better."

"Glad to hear it, love. So what do you want to do now?"

"I don't care, so long as it's with you..."

The End.

About Stephanie Summers

Stephanie Summers is a wife and mother of two. She graduated from West Virginia University with a degree in accounting, though writing is her true passion. Stephanie seemed to always have a story or two or ten running around in her mind. At the ripe old age of 30, she finally decided it was time to put aside the thought that she didn't have what it took to write a novel and began writing her first story.

Craving is the first installment in the Willow Creek Vampires Series, followed by Haunting and Awakening. Her short story, Love Forgotten, was chosen to be published in Stardust: A Futuristic Romance Collection. Her contemporary rock star romance, Take Me On, was released in July 2015, with the sequel, Take Me Home, set to release late 2015. Be sure to check out her erotic short story, Saved by the Bear, available now.

Links to check out:

http://eepurl.com/PWB0P - Sign up for my newsletter

www.facebook.com/authorstephaniesummers - Check out my Facebook page for teaser chapters, contests, and to keep up-to-date on my latest projects.

https://www.tsu.co/StephanieSummers

www.authorstephaniesummers.com

www.twitter.com/authorsasummers

12-16

DISCARD

CPSIA information can be obtained
at www.ICGtesting.com
Printed in the USA
LVOW04s1431181116
513601LV00008B/355/P